THE OTHER KINGDOM

THE OTHER KINGDOM

Victor Price

BREAKAWAY BOOKS
NEW YORK CITY
1996

Published by Breakaway Books
P. O. Box 1109
Ansonia Station
New York, NY 10023
(212) 595-2216

ISBN: 1-55821-451-8

Originally published by Doubleday & Co., Inc.

AUTHOR'S NOTE

When I first wrote this novel, in 1962, I placed the action five years in the future in order to avoid references to living runners. The predictions regarding mile times and training methods for 1967-68 turned out to be satisfyingly accurate, for which I am grateful to James Duthie, who gave his professional help.

Now that future has become the past, with its own characteristic flavour which in my opinion it would be wrong to tamper with. So, in this otherwise fairly extensive rewrite, I have left the entire technical side of the novel unaltered.

Chapter 1

I

Late in September 1967, running on the grass track at Cherryvale, Colin Warnock had his first taste of inspiration. Because inspiration it undoubtedly was, as he recognised in the aftermath. At the time it was merely a sort of trance, a disembodiment.

It was seven days after his twenty-first birthday, and the clock of St Jude's had struck the third quarter after four. The sun, mellow now from the lateness of the hour and of the season, slanted down from above the brick villas of the Ravenhill Road. It had been a dry month, and the mown grass blades stood up crisply as though stiffened with rime: they looked forward to winter.

He was running a half-mile with Foley and Hunter; Jock, their trainer, watched them from the start and finish line, stop-watch in hand. They always trained together, these three, although they specialised in different events. Rex Hunter was a four-forty man and Warnock himself a miler; only Brendan Foley was running in his own race. For the track athlete it is important to go outside one's own province, to supplement natural gifts with inculcated ones: speed with stamina, stamina with speed.

Colin had started the run with his mind on nothing in particular. His thoughts flitted from Beth to his dead father and on to the rooks that circled chattering around their colony in the adjoining trees. He was not really concentrating as they ran the first semi-circle of two hundred and twenty yards. Hunter, big and rangy with crew-cut ash blond hair, an international rugby footballer at the age of twenty, devoured the ground in front of him with his sweeping stride. Ingrained habits die hard: he could not prevent himself taking the lead, running free.

Foley was tucked in behind him: Foley with his thin hawk's face and bent head. His very style of running suggested a monkish shuffle. He ran, as it were, away from sin and always crossed himself before and after a race. He was supposed to offer up his running to Saint Teresa of Lisieux.

Five yards behind Foley Colin loosely loped. His thoughts were still on the rookery when they reached the end of the back straight and began the long turn left; the birds were falling away behind his right shoulder. He came to himself with the thought: after all, I *am* on the track; threw up his chin, and dropped into a firmer stride.

That was when the inspiration came, quite unbidden. Halfway round the top bend he felt a surge of energy. All things were suddenly possible; then what was possible became necessary. He was full of running, inexhaustibly full—but he must set about exhausting the inexhaustible. He was penetrated with an intense joy.

He glided past Foley and then Hunter as if in a dream. Once on his own, with only the track in front of him, he was transported into a region of purer air, a sphere in which brute competition was transcended. His physical functions were no longer a part of him, he felt; his body was rather a machine that ran independently, the heart pumping blood, the lungs seething oxygen, the legs pounding like pistons. He need make no effort; the field of gravity was tilted by a right angle. He merely allowed himself to fall forward and be caught every quarter-second by one of the forward-falling feet. It was his first experience of undiluted happiness or—as Schuhmacher might have put it—heroism.

Starting the second lap, he was aware of a strange look in Jock's eyes as he sailed past. One of those shaggy, hooded eyebrows which made him look like a tired eagle was raised.

He flew around again, hardly aware of what was happening to him, and finished in an even burst of speed that carried him past the trainer by a good twenty yards. He was turning round, laughing, exhilarated, to shout something at Foley and Hunter as they laboured home forty yards behind, when he realised he couldn't breathe. A ton weight was pressing on his rib-case, his head was drained of blood. He sat down abruptly, fighting for breath. His ears rang.

Foley passed the line in a flurry of low strides and slowed, dropping his elbows, his chest flung forward. His breathing was harsh, but even now his lips appeared pursed and tight. He shot Colin a glimpse of timid congratulation.

"Jesus Christ, these halves will be the death of me!" shouted Hunter, expelling his breath in a huge pant and snatching fresh air in lungfulls. "What came over you, Warnock? You were like a greyhound with mustard up its behind." He flung himself unconcernedly on the grass, a man at home with his body. Foley walked off to find his kit with precise, modest steps.

"Have you no sense?" Jock was bustling across to them on his bandy legs. "Into your track suits and no nonsense. Brendan is the only one of you with an ounce of wit. And in the name o' God keep moving! Do you want to seize up like a pair of old motor cars?"

Hunter got quickly to his feet, flexing his biceps. "Fancy me as Mr Universe?" he called to the word in general. Receiving no answer, he sauntered across to the old wooden bench they had dragged out into the middle of the expanse of grass, took his track suit from it and put it on. He was breathing easily again.

Colin followed suit. As he walked, Jock eyed him narrowly from under his mass of grey hair; he had a fine gnarled head with a strong chin and a protruding lower lip, a head that belied his origins in a Glasgow slum. Then his glance fell in unbelief to the stop-watch.

A breath of wind was cooling the sweat on Colin's temples. He could hear Hunter throwing some jibe at Foley as Jock began: "Colin lad, what possessed you there? You did that last lap in fifty seconds flat. Son, if you'd been runnin' from the start you'd have been inside the Irish All-Comers, maybe even the World. And on grass!"

Colin smiled at him in bewilderment. His breath was still coming in gasps. "Do you really think . . . ?" he began. "I knew I was going well, but not like that . . . I'm not an eight-eighty man anyway . . . Funny thing was, it was easy. No effort involved."

"Maybe that's why you're still pechin'" Jock retorted. "I'm tellin' you: you'd have been inside one-forty-four. Do that at a meeting and you'll find yoursel' the world record holder."

Warnock's blue eyes clouded over; he felt suddenly giddy. Jock shook his head. "Just my bleddy luck," he said with assumed asperity. "I wait twenty years for a real runner, and then what happens? His first world-class time scares hell out o' him. Man, you should be happy, happy! Too much imagination, that's your trouble. Too much bleddy imagination."

Warnock said nothing but his thoughts were easily read. They were circling, hypnotised, round the problem of recreating this ecstasy on the world's cold terms. Before the public's indifferent eye, observed and catalogued by the measurers and ratifiers with their small silver watches, how could he ever do it? And with the yapping pack of his competitors around him?

"Perk up," said Jock, taking him by the shoulders. "God Almighty, you've just done the fastest six hundred yards ever. Son, you'll make my fortune yet. Reproduce that form next week and the Yanks'll be knocking each other down to make me offers." He poked Warnock playfully in the chest. "Just chain that imagination to the door post when you come out in the morning and I'll make an Olympic champion of you. Man, you're a natural: legs like steel rods, lungs like a blacksmith's bellows and a heart beat of fifty-two at rest. You were made to cover the ground faster than anybody else. Only you think too much, and that could be your downfall. Don't let it, laddie. Don't let it."

Warnock's mind was trying to cope with the fact that he was capable of great performances—not in the unspecified future, but now. Until ten minutes ago he had merely been "promising"; the redemption of that promise, although very real to him, was too far off to worry about. It was a cosy state; but now his moment of inspiration had happened, barring for ever the road to that comfortable country. He was like a golfer whose handicap has been lowered by observant powers; he could never play off the old easy mark again. Not even in the routine world of club meetings: the press would somehow get to know of this training time of his and step up its demands. He felt sudden resentment at journalists. It was bad enough feeling dissatisfied in your own mind, but now he would lose his rags of public comfort as well.

He was in his track-suit now, hot and clammy. He took off his training shoes with their dimpled soles—Jock made a ceremony of wearing spikes, reserving them for competition—and walked barefoot to the pavilion. Foley and Hunter had gone before, Foley trotting along with a discreet jumpiness, as though he half expected someone to leap out at him, Hunter laughing and gesticulating.

"Anyway," said Jock, picking up his first aid kit and bottle of wintergreen, "if you cannae take your mind off Santry, at least don't get up in the air. Don't keep asking yourself: Can I or can't I? Just think of all those films of Kaufmann and Horvath you've seen. You know their strengths and weaknesses better than I do: concentrate on that. Kaufmann's a runner and Horvath's a racer. The one'll run you off your feet and the other'll bamboozle you. But you've the ability to handle them both—and you're the home boy, remember. That gives you a ten-yard start."

"People mustn't expect too much."

"Balls to what people expect. If they don't get it that needn't worry *you*. Chain up that bleddy imagination, I tell you. Now I'm away home." He took his bicycle from where he had stood it against the pavilion wall and mounted it. The machine trundled out at the gate, propelled by his bulging calves towards his semi-detached house on an estate by the river Lagan, a mile and a half away.

As he pedalled his mind ran on Colin's second lap. It was hard to repress a pang of excitement: Warnock was the sort of athletic material every coach dreams of getting his hands on, his chance in life.

That six hundred yards now: it was bonny, as bonny as anything he had seen. Half a lap of dawdling and then the lad had cut loose, falling into the cadence of a very fast quarter without losing any of that long-legged grace that singled him out. Jock had half expected that he would blow up, but no: he had carried on through the last lap in that suspended state that a sprinter calls his float and then given his last dregs of energy to stage a finish. A sprint you couldn't call it, but then such things were illusory nowadays; when your stamina is at breaking point you can't sprint, you can only resist deceleration.

As he freewheeled between the red frontages of the Ormeau Road, he thought back to the first time he had seen the lad. Would he ever forget it? Inter-school sports, four years ago in June. Warnock was one of the names he had scrawled in his notebook; so, curiously enough, was Foley. But Colin was the fellow he was really looking out for—the VC's boy to begin with, and a big school reputation into the bargain. Warnock, lankier and more unformed than now but with the same easy movement, had strode away from the other milers and coasted home in a record time. Jock shrugged as he put a pencil ring round his name, thinking: he's probably booked for Oxford anyway.

But Warnock was not booked for Oxford. He had stayed in Ireland and run for him. Always in the same way: killing the mediocre opposition before the bell and coming home aloof and withdrawn. Jock had never seen him exhaust himself till this very afternoon.

"Aye, and that's just the trouble!" he muttered between his teeth; he was turning left, into the embankment. "You can't play the bleddy aristocrat in this game." Not if you wanted to get anywhere, that is. Warnock had merely been serving his time till now; even his four-minute mile last summer was prentice work. At Santry he would be thrown in with two mature men, masters of their trade; no chance of running such into the ground. Only a combination of speed, strength and cunning would do.

Jock looked forward to the race with gusto and apprehension. Warnock had it in him to produce a great performance, of that he was sure. Not necessarily a winning one, although he had hopes of that too. A second, even a third, in such company could be a triumph if it was gained in the right way and the time was good. It all depended on the lad's psychology.

"Christ, I'm gettin' as bad as he is," he thought with a quirk of humour. It wasn't his way to gnaw at worry like a dog at an old bone. It never had been. He was a slum kid, a product of the Gorbals with no time for hair-splitting or self-questioning. At the age when Warnock was winning his school miles his only problem had been to keep clear of the razors.

It was the war that engineered his escape. Thrown into uniform in 1940, when he was eighteen, he had found himself one afternoon on a grassless football field, bawled at by a rubber-necked instructor. He hated football, so asked to be considered for athletics instead: it could scarcely be worse than getting kicked, knocked over and then shouted at for your pains.

To his and everyone else's surprise he turned out to be a fine quarter-miler, boring along on his powerful little legs, running head down like an enraged ox but covering the distance in less than forty-nine seconds at a time when nobody else in the war-disrupted country was capable of that.

So, eventually, he became the rubber-necked instructor himself, the P.T.I. sergeant who after the war found his way to this Irish university and to this tight little semi at which he was now dismounting, a coach who made a decent enough living but had to hold his tongue when the Stampfls, the Ceruttys and the Lydiards spoke. But maybe after Santry . . . It would be a laugh if the interviewers made for the Gorbals kid for once.

Thank the Lord his problems had always been of the earth, earthy: how to drag himself out of the gutter, how to put a bite in his bairns' mouths. Having none of such, Warnock invented his own. And the invented ones were worse than the ready-made.

Jock Campbell was no despiser of intellect; he was too much the Scot not to have a certain reverence for it. But he was glad he hadn't been born to it. He could take the direct route to an object, not be circumvented by the twists of his own brain. And yet, he suddenly thought, who could say if the winding road mightn't go further in the long run?

Meanwhile, in the steaming bath, Colin Warnock looked at his legs, lightly flecked with black hairs, wobbling under six inches of water. The bending of light rays made them seem to float just under the surface, two-dimensional and fragile. It was hard to have much confidence in them.

II

Beth McCann was whirled through the wayside station at fifty-five miles an hour as the train hauled itself up to its cruising speed and, having got there, settled to a comfortable mile a minute. Four times faster than man when, years ago, he had flung himself at the hypothetical four-minute barrier.

The rhythm of the wheels answered her mood. Long weeks at home, longed for before they came, had developed into a greater strain than strain itself. That febrile clackety-clack soothed and excited her at the same time. She perched forward on the dusty moquette, scorning the back rest. Her eyes travelled erratically from feature to feature of the unrolling landscape: a liver-and-white cow; a potato-digger tossing up earth full of stalks and tubers, its spikes going round like a revolving porcupine; a farmer's wife taking in her washing; a cat whisking round the corner of a barn. Through the windows on the other side the sea flashed slate-grey, the colour of her eyes.

Each time she turned her head her remarkable black hair, which grew out without a parting from the crown and was cut straight across on nape and forehead, swung like something living. It was so fine and yet so abundant that from anywhere but close up you could not see the individual hairs; the whole dark growth was homogeneous as a piece of velvet.

On the seat beside her was a paper-backed book, a serious work on the contemporary French novel, bought in Belfast and brought home as holiday reading, but left unopened till today. Would she read it now? No, she would not.

She loved these moments of transition. Her parents had driven her to Limavady station in the Jaguar and would have continued all the way to Belfast, but she wouldn't have it. She would not be denied the train journey, with its opportunities for letting the imagination loose. She was a human projectile fired by the Limavady world at the city and its people. People like Warnock.

It was a relief to abandon her role as crown princess of a country town, installed by her grandfather's money and anointed by universal respect. Her father was the most important man in the place and a power in the County Council, proprietor of half the main street, Worshipful Master of the Masonic lodge and owner of the big house overlooking the river, with its rockeries, greenhouses and parasols on the lawn. The expensive car stood carelessly in front of it.

The passionate side of her nature came from him, but where he channelled his energies into the little town, stamping it with his trade mark, hers was dissipated round her, blown off like steam that drives no turbines. Now that she was being carried away from him he seemed more admirable than when she was with him: the willpower, with its hint of ruthlessness, that kept him where he was in the town, was softened and more attractively lit. The saving humour came out more strongly. She felt a moment of homesickness for his square face, lined now and with a small brush of moustache, for the thinning hair that had been like hers.

The face she had inherited too; it was too square for a women's magazine, and too determined. But she had no quarrel with it.

From her mother came her figure but nothing else she could discover. That kind but obscure personality was a recessive gene, plunging into oblivion only to turn up, perhaps, in some placid great-grandchild in the twenty-first century.

Yes, she was her father's child all right. All save her eyes, which were grey and uneasy, the eyes of some animal that had crept in from the wild Gaelic landscape that lurks on the outskirts of every Ulster town. They betrayed the fact that she was highly-sexed but too proud to resort to casual satisfaction. Oh, she had experimented all right, but boys were such clumsy creatures! Then, on holiday two years ago, she had fallen in with an altogether tougher specimen. He half-forced, half-seduced her and made her realise an important truth about herself: she was fastidious, a lady. She could only give herself to the right man. In Colin Warnock she thought she had found that man.

What drew her to him was his brooding quality; she sensed that his self-discipline covered a temperament as passionate as her own. He had fires all right, but they were banked and burning deep down. The element of secrecy and withdrawal was repeated in his physical appearance. Like many athletes he was unremarkable in his ordinary clothes: just another tall young man with dark hair. But stripped for running he had a kind of elegant leanness, with slim muscles that leaped under the skin. Early that summer she had been to a swimming party and picnic given by the university German Society. Colin was there; she had a whole afternoon to examine him. His chest was broad and somewhat shallow, but with slabs of breast-muscle; it had been a effort not to touch him. Thank God she hadn't though; with that kind of boy you never knew. He might have shied off for good. Sitting beside him in the bus home, she had felt that her restraint had been in some way rewarded, that there was a kind of understanding between them. If only he would act on it!

Thinking of that day she shivered slightly, then noticed that a middle-aged man in the seat opposite was sliding a furtive gaze from her breasts to her calves. She stared at him and changed seats with a haughty air.

It was sickening to be looked at in that way. To be offered, however obliquely, raddled flesh you didn't want was intolerable because it cast doubts on the sweetness of the flesh you did. She closed her eyes, penetrated by her need for Colin. It was not just a physical need; she longed to give her whole personality to him, to wrap him in her warmth. His long face with its vertical lines and deep-set eyes was still the face of a boy; it was easy to persuade herself that he needed her too.

Every sixty seconds carried her a mile nearer to the flat that overlooked the tennis courts at Windsor Avenue, a flat once shared but now, since her girl-friend's wedding, hers alone. It was part of a converted house, with two or three levels linked by short staircases. She had put chintz curtains at the windows and furnished it in an old-fashioned, feminine way, full of flower-patterned armchair covers. From this den she could look down on the bronzed tennis players banging the ball, pleasing her with their noise.

Thinking of the to-and-fro of tennis balls brought her mind back to the train; she let herself fall into its urgent rhythm. It was bringing her to the more urgent life of the city, and she liked having her thoughts brought forward, she liked living in the future.

III

Colin went to the Union at nine o'clock. He was restless, looking for something to do. A figure was stretched out horizontal on one of the scuffed leather armchairs in the reading room: Sam Harbinson. "Care for a game?" asked Warnock.

Harbinson followed him into the billiard room without a word; there was a table free. The caretaker, a retired military man who regarded his charges as a regimental sergeant-major regards youthful subalterns, put on the light for them.

Harbinson said his first word as they were chalking their cues. "For the table, eh?" He had one of those Ballymena voices that don't intend to give anything away.

"All right, but give me a few points up. I'm not a pool-room shark like you."

Harbinson raised his eyebrows, which gave him a ferocious look. "Thirty in the hundred," he said curtly.

Warnock accepted, thinking: I might as well pay in advance. Possessing money of his own, he found it undignified to argue over it.

"Go ahead," said Harbinson. Colin played and left the balls safe, with the red in baulk.

"Clever boy." He raised his eyebrows again; years ago he had done it deliberately, for effect; now it was a habit. Taking his cue, he bent over the cloth, his head in the stark white pyramid of light. His attempt at a three-cushion cannon missed by half an inch.

Colin's turn. The baize was startling green under the light; with your head down you saw nothing of what went on away from the table. It was soothing to be there, bent over this miniature football field with its worn patches at the D and the red-spot. The harshness of the light lent the game importance—mock importance, you knew, but you accepted the simplistic scheme of values while you were inside that brilliant box. It was like a running track, only here you could have triumphs without self-sacrifice. He tried for an in-off red and missed.

Harbinson played. He was tall and thin, like Colin himself,

but unhealthily so, almost emaciated. His complexion was compounded of the dust of billiard halls and betting shops, a leathery yellow in colour. Insofar as he was anything, he was a professional gambler.

But he could handle a cue! "Tricky one here," he said carelessly and Warnock watched him strike the cue-ball with heavy left-hand side. The little white sphere cracked against the red one and followed through, before spinning off the cushion and nudging Warnock's ball: a virtuoso cannon.

"Good shot."

Sam grunted, then potted the red the length of the table. It dropped with a heavy clunk, but he was dissatisfied; his own ball had ended too far from the others.

"Nothing on this time," Warnock ventured.

"In that case . . ." Harbinson gave the ball a mighty hit, sending both it and the red flying round the table. With its dying strength the cue ball hit Warnock's and dribbled into the centre pocket.

"Brute force and ignorance," said Warnock.

"The only way out of an intellectual quandary. Better than farting around puzzling it out." He was rarely as talkative as this, but even with his tongue loosened he sounded laconic.

His next shot was easy, but he missed it. He raised his eyebrows again and chalked his cue vigorously, as though to punish it. "How's the athletic prowess?" he asked suddenly.

Warnock, caught off guard, blurted out: "I did a good time today. Up to world standard, Jock said."

"Hope it makes you happy." Harbinson cleared his throat noisily, took out a handkerchief and ejected the phlegm into it; he was a martyr to catarrh.

They moved round the table for a while, saying nothing, like wraiths. The world was dark outside the wedges of light, and beyond the Union building nothing existed at all. Warnock's thirty-point lead melted away. He had a good eye and a steady hand, but seldom played because the smoky atmosphere made him fear for his wind. Athletes are touchy about unimportant things.

He went ahead again with a good slender in-off white. The balls lined up for a cannon of moderate difficulty, which he brought off; then he potted the red.

"When d'your lectures start?" Harbinson grunted.

"Tuesday. Not that it matters. Only old Schuhmacher has anything to say. And yours?"

"Have done already."

"You been to any?"

"No." Warnock looked at him enquiringly. "Why should I?" said Harbinson with unaccustomed heat. "Who wants to spend his life in a ruddy law office? I'll get a man in and share profits on a fifty-fifty basis when the oul fella kicks off."

So saying, he played a neat little break. Warnock was enveloped in the soothing click of billiard balls; at the counter the retired military man was favouring a captive youth with his wartime experiences. Poor fellow, he'd only come in to buy a packet of cigarettes.

"I hear you're running on Saturday week," said Harbinson, the break over.

Warnock rested his cue on the bridge of thumb and forefinger and examined the lie of the balls. "Yes," he said slowly. "Dublin. The Santry meeting, last of the season. They're bringing over a couple of foreign runners for me to compete with."

"I know. Kaufmann and Horvath."

"You've heard of them?"

"I read my papers." Colin played his shot; the red banged into the pocket. "The scribes say it'll be your first run against world-class opposition. The acid test, they say."

Colin potted the red again, skillfully, bringing all three balls together so that, theoretically at least, he could continue making tip-tap cannons indefinitely.

"Not bad, son," said Harbinson, his brows up again. "But let's see what you make of it."

Colin made two cannons, then touched his cue ball a shade too definitely. The triangle was pulled out of shape; one more cannon and the automatic break would be over.

"Stick to the cinders, old son," said Harbinson, grinning ghoulishly, and embarked on a fifty-break with which he won the game. All Warnock had to do from that point on was stand by the scoreboard, moving the little brass tally as the points mounted.

The first stroke was a combined cannon and pot-red. Having achieved it, Sam stood with his cue lightly balanced between his finger-tips, the end resting on the baize. "You seem to like old Schuhmacher," he said.

In-off red. "He was a friend of my father's, you know. And his family knew my mother's people in Leipzig."

"Funny old bugger."

Short cannon, lining up for pot-red. "How do you mean?"

"Remember that time he spoke here?"

Red in pocket, cue ball slightly out of line. "Oh yes." Colin remembered all right. The student debating society had invited the Professor of German to speak in the hall downstairs. The motion was one of those off-handed undergraduate affairs: "That this house prefers an age without a name." Schuhmacher had spoken against. "How come you knew about that? You're not the debating type."

Lips pursed, Sam considered the recovery shot. "Couldn't get a game. Dunwoody was talking. Making them laugh. So I came down."

A lovely gliding in-off, bringing the red well down the table for the bread and butter shot: in-off to the centre pocket.

"Your prof spoke well," said Warnock. Dunwoody, the law professor, was a florid man with the pouting lips of a Roman emperor, a master of the cultivated witticism. While he spoke Schuhmacher had sat perfectly still, one raised hand holding his silver propelling pencil between thumb and forefinger, like a dart. How could he possibly make a valid reply to this civilised persiflage?

"Not when he's lecturing," said Harbinson. "In case you're trying to get me to attend."

Ball in pocket, with a little plop of finality. "Don't worry."

"Still, that old nut-case of yours made a good come-back." The praise was grudging, as though he was admitting to owing somebody money.

"Yes, he did rather." Remarkably, Schuhmacher had dispelled all doubts from the start: the metallic precision of his English, the clipped text-book voice, cut straight through Dunwoody's woolly urbanity, temporarily imposing his own peculiar world-view. Indeed he had made a curiously impressive figure as he stood there in his incongruous tweeds, his chin a permanent blue-black, a hank of grizzled hair pulled over his bald pate, saying his piece with as little emotion as if it had been a scholarly paper.

"Mind you, it was a lot of rubbish."

Another in-off red. "That's a matter of opinion." Schuhmacher had given his audience a precis of his numerous books: the death of heroism implied by the motion was an established fact. An unfortunate one, because men had discovered that they could not be happy without it. Much of the literature produced since the romantic period was a conscious attempt to win it back, to regain what he called the heroic posture. Schuhmacher was not afraid of big words.

"Humph."

Five further in-offs, during which they said nothing. Through the soporific click of the balls Colin recalled the professor's actual words: "In attempting the heroic we are merely trying to realise our human potential."

Sam foozled the last in-off but compensated with a cannon which brought the balls together at the top of the table. The break was already worth thirty-two. "Hand me the rest, will you?" With his cue in the angle of the stubby-armed St Andrew's cross, he stroked his ball across the table. Thirty-five.

Heaven alone knew what the adolescents sitting in the hall had thought of Schuhmacher's performance. What might the heroic posture mean to them? Something sexual perhaps. But Warnock knew it was the distillation of the professor's intellectual life and felt it was important to himself, perhaps because of his German blood, certainly because of his position as his father's son. As for ordinary Ulster boys and girls brought up on thrift and hard work, porridge and potatoes, he couldn't begin to guess.

Three rapid pot-reds, the third executed with screw-back, followed by a cannon: forty-six.

"Fellas like that make your life a misery," said Sam unexpectedly. "And you only have it once." He potted the red again; his points tally was now ninety-eight.

"Gimme the chalk, will you?" He renewed the green on the point of his cue and walked to the other end of the table with hunched shoulders. Eyebrows lifting again, he said "How about something nice to finish with?" Ignoring an easy in-off white, he made his ball clip the red before rolling down the table and back again, via the side cushion. Finally it trickled up to Warnock's, touched it and won the game. "Well, that's that," he said. "How about another?"

"I must be off home. If I'm to get my regulation ten hours sleep."

"See you then."

"See you."

As Warnock walked away he heard the sharp mid-Antrim voice: "Don't forget to pay on your way out."

Outside, the last warmth of summer lingered. He turned into the shadowy quadrangle under the archway and crossed obliquely to the rear of the main entrance. A breath of air stirred in the cherry trees; the only light was from a single window opposite where someone in the History Department was working late.

Inside the entrance hall strip-lighting fell on yellow-washed walls with dark wooden beams and blue doors. A permanent gusty breeze flapped the papers on the notice boards. He passed through, then out past the war memorial with its winged angel to the University Road, whirring with cars. He crossed over at the church and turned through the gateway—now destitute of gates—into College Gardens. He had lived there once. Indeed the school that he, and Sam, had attended stood on a little height to the left. *Situs in monticulo*, as the school song said.

Here was the house in which he had lived as a small boy: three high-ceilinged storeys, a warren of rooms that excluded the sun in varying degrees, the whole Victorian terrace mouldy and impractical but with a damp dignity. It was here that his father, Robert Warnock, had first become a person to him and not an enigmatic but friendly-disposed giant. Here he had the shattering realisation that he was the son of a great man. He remembered what Schuhmacher had said once: "All intelligent young men rebel against their fathers."

That was just Schuhmacher of course, generalising from the particular to make it more palatable. And he was *not* in rebellion against his father; rather he admired him to excess. But he felt oppressed by his size and weight. How was it possi-

27

ble to achieve an identity of his own in that enormous shadow?

He walked on. To the left, on the Field (the boys, in their exclusive way, gave it a capital letter) where he had played touch-rugby, there were new classroom blocks, already drab. It was there, when he was fourteen, that he had first realised he was an athlete. A master had made the whole class run round the pitch, again and again. To Warnock's astonishment he found himself still running after everybody else—his heroes included—had either dropped out or was hobbling half a lap behind. He couldn't understand it. Surely they were foxing, or just didn't care? He was scarcely out of breath himself and attached no importance to his feat. But to the others he had suddenly become a person of interest, and this unexpected eminence finally convinced him.

His thoughts had brought him to the Lisburn Road, where he boarded an out-bound bus, climbing the stairs to have peace to think. Curious how that silly little triumph, gained in ignorance of its value, had changed his life! It had taken him from a state of numb indifference to one in which some kind of hope was possible. Of course it meant losing the bleak security of rock-bottom—or most of it; the last traces had lingered until that very afternoon. Now they were gone for good. Like it or not, he was committed. A practical sense of honour demanded that he prove himself, in his own way, worthy of the name he had been born to.

The bus dropped him at Balmoral Avenue. He walked along the broad, ill-lit street lined with trees to the house he lived in, a house so instinct with his father's personality that he refused to leave it when made Vice-Chancellor. He could not be prevailed upon to move into the Lodge; "Let the mountain come to Mohammed," he had said in his still-strong North Down accent, tossing his mane of white hair.

How typical of the man! Typical of his size, his solidity, of the immense assurance with which he inhabited his world. It was that assurance that made him "great"—a quality hard to pin down but too large to be called arrogant. There was too much simplicity, even a kind of humility about it: he was a man who *knew*, knew the relative importance of people and things, knew without pretension that he himself occupied a place higher than most of the others and acted accordingly. When they offered him the customary knighthood he exploded with indignant laughter. "*Sir?*—What does *sir* mean? And don't talk to me of Lord Crawfordsburn or Baron Belfast. Would you condemn me to anonymity? No, I'll stay plain Mister Robert Warnock. Everybody knows who that is."

His son, no expert on world nutrition, turned in at the gate of his house.

IV

It was the first Tuesday in October. They sat dutifully on their wooden benches, spoil of some long defunct school, waiting for Schuhmacher to begin. Outside, the sun had vanished and there was a nip of autumn in the air. No turning back now; the year was striding towards the finish.

Warnock was in the second row, not too far back to appear a philistine and not too far forward to seem a toady; it was the only possible position for a known friend of the professor.

The German Department was in a house in a Victorian terrace, once favoured by doctors but now bought up almost entirely by the university for its poorer and less prestigious departments. The high sash windows, running on cords in the old style, overlooked the Students' Union and the Gothic

29

extravaganza that housed the library. The room had the super-annuated dignity that goes with moulded ceilings and chandeliers, but it was a dignity under assault: a naked bulb hung from the central rose of the ceiling and a blackboard had been screwed to one wall. The only furnishings were these ancient benches, gnarled with carved names, plus an old pitch-pine lectern behind which Schuhmacher now stood, going through the opening ceremony they knew so well.

He was always preceded into the room by a red register, more apt for a school than a university, containing the names and class marks of his students; on this were balanced the three or four books, marked by paper spills, which he needed for his lecture; his spectacle case, fountain pen and propelling pencil; and a small red cigarette tin containing pieces of chalk. He had never been known to carry any of these objects in his pockets.

All these belongings he arranged meticulously on the lectern: the register and books on the sloping surface, the rest on the flat top part with its two chiselled grooves: pen and pencil into the grooves themselves, chalk and glasses case squared off to their right. Then his well-manicured, rather feminine right hand would dive into his trouser fob, produce an old silver hunter watch which he laid carefully to the right of the glasses case.

Having done that he closed his dark eyes, which seemed all pupil, and held his finger tips together as if in prayer.

The nudges and winks the closed eyes provoked stopped abruptly when they were opened again. Schuhmacher looked deliberately round the room and began to speak.

"I have called this series of lectures *The Literature Of Strain*—yes, Johnson, that is also the title of a book of mine—and in it will deal principally with Hölderlin, Kleist and Nietzsche. These men, I would argue, have made the most characteristic and valuable contribution of modern German writers to the literature of the world." As always, he commanded attention. The pale Jewish face, permanently blue with the beard under the skin—no razor could make any impression on it; the clipped metallic voice; even the casual tweeds he affected, had a kind of magnetism about them.

"What do I mean by *strain*? Something more than mere tension; a straining *after*, with an element of overreaching about it. What it is straining after will become apparent. For the moment let us merely say that it is after something which thoughtful men have not been vouchsafed since the Enlightenment: call it God, if you like. But it would be more accurate to describe it as man's relationship to God. Our three writers were in search of a relationship with the Final Cause which would amount to more than the narrow satisfaction of the needs of human nature: they sought the total realisation of their human *potential*."

The idea was familiar to Warnock from a dozen books and the conversation of years. He stopped listening and looked at Beth.

She was sitting on the same bench as he was, separated from him by an anonymous girl in a mackintosh; her dark head was propped on her hand. She was wearing a thick woollen pullover that seemed all of a piece, the colour of cognac, and had pushed the sleeves up as far as her elbows. The bosom was enhanced by draping, the fore-arms by being bare. He realised that was not the only one to feel how desirable she was, and suppressed a pang of resentment.

She and he had one of those indefinite relationships which are the product of inexperience; each was attracted and knew instinctively that the other was attracted too, but nothing was said. Warnock realised that the fault was his but had not the courage to remedy it. Yet he expected her to behave as though under an obligation to him, and was angry when she didn't!

Once, in a cinema lobby, he had seen her with a medical student who had wound his blue scarf round his neck and tossed one end over his shoulder; the shock of sexual jealousy was all the stronger in that he himself was a virgin.

". . . we may with justification paraphrase La Bruyère and say: Everything has been *done* and we are too late on the scene. This is the problem which has proved so fatal for the over-reacher, the man who aspires to do things on the heroic scale. Human opportunities have dwindled, but the human race has not; it still throws up the same proportion of heroic temperaments, of men like Kleist and Nietzsche. You note that I define heroism as a cast of mind. I discount the dynamism of mere military adventurers. Beethoven is, after all, a greater man than Napoleon."

Beth's eyelashes flickered. She found it difficult to hold a tranquil pose. Ripples ran over her small square face, tiny shadows cast by some surface muscle as she frowned in concentration. She tossed her head; the dark burnish moved with it. Warnock felt her tug powerfully at him. Why had he not written to her during the holidays, or phoned her since term started? He had no answers to these questions and could only lament his own indecision, which had limited their relationship to a few hundred surreptitious glances, a score or two of cups of coffee and one single afternoon on the beach.

". . . *Belief* is the essential climate of heroism, but belief was swept away by the tidal wave of scientific humanism born of the Renaissance. As Nietzsche put it, God is dead. Now however you define God, He is clearly an outward goal towards which men can strive. Destroy that goal and the heroic mind has to find something to replace it: something within itself."

Her grey eyes slid past Colin, halting for a moment on his face. Did he imagine it, or was there the nervous ghost of a smile? Then she swivelled round to look out the window, seemed dissatisfied with that, swung back again and stared Schuhmacher in the eye, as if daring him to continue; but he was blandly indifferent to the challenge.

Warnock thought back to the first time he had seen her. It was at an evening meeting of the German Society a year ago when a music lecturer, a dapper brown-haired man, came to talk about Richard Strauss and play his records on the Society's battered gramophone (they hadn't the money to take the plunge into the hi-fi age). She had stared at the speaker with the same nervous challenge as now, had fidgeted as now. Warnock had felt a sudden urge to soothe her, to calm her, but of course did nothing of the kind. Natural, spontaneous behaviour did not come easy to him; something in him, a baffled sense of vocation perhaps, stilted his actions as they were conceived. Only on the track was self-expression possible.

". . . in the age of belief the only permitted knowledge was that of God. But the men of the Renaissance wrested knowledge away from the Deity and applied it to man himself. *The proper study of mankind is man*: that is the conclusion to which the humble study of a few worm-eaten manuscripts inevitably led. Self-knowledge, in other words. But the fledgling self-knowledge was soon tossed out of the nest by a monstrous cuckoo: self-*consciousness*. What it tossed out was spontaneous life; or so the Romantics discovered."

He had never had an evening alone with her. Once they had found themselves in a party of four at a concert given by a visiting orchestra. The large cold hall was dominated by the gilded statue of a previous monarch. They had arrived just as the doors were closing and sat down in some confusion, Beth and Colin separated by the other two. Colin, no great psychologist, sensed that there was tension between the other man, Humphreys, and his girl. He had clearly called Warnock in to help through an awkward date, and the girl had done the same with Beth. The four of them sat through the music as if condemned to it. Finally it was over: a clatter of upended seats, a hurried shuffle towards the doors.

"Where to now?" said Humphreys when they were safely outside.

Colin: "Perhaps we might . . ."

Beth: "Coffee. I'm thirsty. First bus into town."

Other Girl: "All right."

Colin (making a panicky bid for Beth): "Let's break up and meet again down town. We'll never get in the same bus."

Other Girl (promptly): No. We'll queue together."

Three quarters of an hour later they were squeezed into a crowded coffee-bar, sitting guiltily around the corpse of the evening, waiting for the moment when they might decently separate. Then further buses carried Beth and the girl off in one direction, Humphreys and Colin in another, in centrifugal flight from their embarrassment.

And that was all he had of her! A few memories, at worst painful, at best equivocal. Yet the flesh-and-blood girl was here beside him, near enough to touch. The sight of her bare forearm, twitching as she wrote in her notebook, decided him: he would speak to her, commit himself to her.

". . . Self-consciousness is essentially the spirit of comparison; men examine their actions in the light of what others have achieved. Small wonder if they are discouraged, when those others are everyone who has ever lived! So, inevitably, we arrive at La Bruyère. He was the first to measure himself against the ancients and find himself wanting. The first to whom the idea occurred; it has occurred to every thinking man since.

"I can hear your mental reservation: surely self-consciousness has always existed? It has indeed. It is the very faculty which has enabled man to transcend his animal state. That is what the Greeks meant by their *gnothi seauton*. But the Greeks stood at the beginning of a era; they were not overpowered by history. With them self-knowledge was the servant, not the master.

"But our great German writers—Hölderlin, Kleist, Nietzsche —stand at the opposite end of history's reversed telescope. They have an overwhelming sense of their own insignificance; for that reason they find the self-knowledge principle an abyss. In these lecturers I shall attempt to plot their course up to, and unfortunately over, the edge of this chasm."

His proemium over, Schuhmacher reached for his notes and started to talk about Hölderlin's life. Outside, the sky was dull, the day windless. The air was in a humid trance, a very Irish phenomenon. The only intrusion of movement was when a yellow leaf detached itself from one of the university horse-chestnuts and fluttered thirty feet to the ground. Warnock sank himself in his resolution: he would speak to Beth. He turned the resolve over and over in his mind until it and the leaf became one, falling endlessly through the grey atmosphere.

Beth came out of the lecture feeling slightly giddy from willing Colin to pay attention to her: to look at her, give her a smile, do anything except listen to Schuhmacher. Schuhmacher was her enemy, the enemy of all women; what weapon had she against male intellectualism except her body? But Warnock seemed uninterested in that, although she had sent its telepathy pulsing along the six feet of desk between them. Now no further appeal was possible; it was up to him.

She walked down the stairs with Patricia Orr, a fair-haired girl with a tendency to blush.

"He was on his hobby horse again, wasn't he?" said Patricia with one of her eager smiles; she had sensed Beth's resentment and was anxious to play to it.

"Don't ask me. You know more about this stuff than I do."

"Och, what you've read doesn't matter. It's just his way of thinking. The boys are always on about it. They say he has a bee in his bonnet about heroism."

Beth tossed her hair back. "He irritates me. Sets my teeth on edge. It's like an allergy. —Oh damn, let's talk about something else."

"Of course." Patricia smiled her nervous smile. "Shall we have a coffee?"

"All right." They walked out the door and across the street, making for the soot-grimed Union. Oh Jesus Christ, let him do something, put me out of my misery, thought Beth. But she refused to turn her head.

Patricia talked her all the way across. And nothing happened. It was eleven o'clock, a popular time; they had to queue. As the line of adolescents advanced she turned her head and saw that Warnock was a few places behind her, with two of the fellows in his year. They were talking with that air of animated authority that men—even immature men—had. Damn men! They had their own world, with a No Admittance notice on the gate. You could get into bed with them, but just you try getting into their minds! Their minds were like their clubs; only certain rooms were open to women.

"Some of these writers are a bit wild and woolly for me," Patricia was saying. "I mean, they're great poets and all that, but don't you get tired of being harrowed?"

They sat down. "God, this coffee's awful," Beth complained. "Sorry, Pat. Hardly the thing to say to the one who bought it. But really, it gets more like stewed acorns every day."

Patricia was intent on her argument. "I mean, all that breast-beating and crying for the moon; it hasn't got much to *say* to us, has it? We can't all be neurotics."

"May I sit here?" Warnock was standing over them, coffee

cup in hand, stooping exaggeratedly because of his height. The colour rushed into Beth's cheeks. Patricia realised their secret; a wave of pink came over her too.

"Please do." Beth said no more; her voice would rise to a terrified shriek if she uttered another word.

"Did you have a good holiday?" Warnock asked, looking at Patricia but meaning her.

But it was Patricia who answered. "I went to my pen-friend in Bordeaux. Sounds daft to have a pen-friend still, but unlike most people we never left off after school." She blabbered on about the pine-resinous Landes, the wine-hills of the Dordogne, the tawny-yellow stream pouring under the bridges of the city to empty itself into the broad sea-wedge of the Gironde.

He turned, at last, to Beth. "How about you?"

"Oh, the usual. Limavady. But we did have three weeks in Dubrovnik." Her hands were tightly folded, in her lap.

"I meant to write." How he got the words out he didn't know; he was fighting an instinctive need to run away, to get clear of uncertainty as he got clear of other runners on the track. He drank a mouthful of coffee.

"That's all right." Please make him stay, God. "What about yourself?"

"As usual with me too. Hamburg, with my mother, for a couple of weeks. Rest of the time, running."

"They've been saying marvellous things about you," blurted Patricia. "The best chance Ulster's ever had of winning an Olympic gold medal—it *is* gold, isn't it?"

Running was another event that took place in the men's rooms. Beth tilted her chin and said: "All sports writers count their chickens before they're hatched. That's what my father says."

In an odd way her scepticism reduced the pressure on him. He looked at her gratefully: her attitude was defiant but the eyes were vulnerable. He was touched.

"Just how good *are* you?" she forced herself to ask. He shrugged in embarrassment, but she insisted. "I mean, is it worth it? The time, the training, the self-denial?"

"I . . . I'm not sure. It might be. I have to go on, in case."

Patricia was looking at him solemnly, her eyes an earnest china-blue. Beth went on: "To make it worthwhile you really have to be good, don't you? Fame is the spur, and all that." She was speaking against Schuhmacher; Colin happened to get in the way.

"I don't think of it that way. It just seems important to make the attempt, to do something really difficult. Like winning at the Olympics."

"Well, are you going to?"

"I did a world-class time in training the other day," he said helplessly.

"I heard about that. Does it mean anything?" Her voice was full of suppressed anger. The mingling of attractiveness and waspishness in her confused him. "It means nothing," he said lamely. "Only competition counts."

"We'll see what it means on Saturday, won't we?" smiled Patricia.

"Yes, you will." He smiled too, but ruefully.

Having hurt him, Beth was full of contrition. God, she thought in panic, don't let me burst into tears or something. She had just enough presence of mind to head the weakness off. "I just don't understand," she said, obliquely apologetic. "Why do people have to prove things to themselves?"

Colin sketched a gesture of renunciation with his hands. Patricia looked at him as though he was the spirit of idealism incarnate, but said nothing: anything she had to say now would be in flat contradiction to what she had opined to Beth five minutes earlier.

As for Beth, her tearfulness was turning to annoyance again. He wasn't going to make a move, clearly. Curse his stupidity, or blindness, or whatever! A single word would put them on the same footing as other people—why on earth didn't he say it? She finished her coffee, stood up and said: "I'm for the library. I have work to do."

"I'll join you," said Patricia. Warnock stood up, awkwardly.

Beth was suddenly tired. She had been concentrating hard and the effort had made her faint. All to no purpose. Warnock mumbled a goodbye, leaving them to make their slow way to the library where, damn it, she hadn't a thing to do. Patricia trailed spaniel-like behind her.

V

Next day Colin was training on his own, surging round the top bend, when Jock's bicycle appeared from behind the gable of the pavilion. He faltered in his stride but finished the lap. The machine rolled along the earth path to him, and they were alone in the grassy emptiness of Cherryvale, plucked at by the light breeze.

"I just happened to be coming by and saw you over the fence." Jock shot out his lower lip. "What are ye up to?"

"I was doing some interval work."

"What work?"

"Quarters."

"What interval?"

Warnock hesitated. "One minute."

"You silly wee bugger! The meeting's in three days. You're supposed to be tapering off. D'ye want to ruin your chances?"

"I . . . just felt I needed it."

"You need what I say you need." Jock glared at him from under his eyebrows. "God give me patience!—Look, son, you know as well as I do that short intervals force your body to make an effort when it's not ready for it. They give you strength—but you don't need strength right now. You *are* strong. What you need is to keep your edge sharp, not lose freshness. Why the hell did you do it?"

Colin said nothing.

Jock smashed his right fist into the palm of his left hand. "Trying to work something out of your system, I'll be bound. Why can't you have a wet dream and forget it?" He was still standing astride the bicycle; he threw his leg over the saddle and let the machine drop. "What sort of a runner have I got on my hands anyway?"

Colin, crestfallen, looked away.

"Look, you know my rule about personal problems: keep them out of your running. And if you can't do that keep out of my way. Is that clear?"

Warnock nodded, overwhelmed by the pointlessness of his own revolt.

"Right then." Jock clapped him on the arm. "Now jog a couple of laps while I get changed."

Colin, relieved, loped round, while Jock divested himself of his track suit, revealing a barrel chest on which ginger hairs stood up like the stuffing of a mattress under the singlet; brawny bow-legs issued from his navy shorts. As Colin passed the starting point for the second time he tagged on. "I'll do a lap with you. Steady striding, mind; I'm at your elbow."

As they ran the older man grunted out advice, the words jolted out of shape as the regular concussions travelled up to his diaphragm.

"Sharpen your stride, but hold it. Last lap: you've just had the bell. From here on only one thing counts—tactics. Forget your training times; just watch. Watch the German. And watch that wee black Hungarian—he'll do you down if he can."

They were turning into the back straight, moving well. "You're under pressure now. Especially if you're feeling strong. You'll want to make your effort—spend the money in the bank. Don't. It's what the Hungarian wants. Not the German; he'll run his own race. Don't go too soon. Don't give Horvath the satisfaction."

Colin listened, demurring mentally at the implied valuation of Horvath. Horvath the diabolical! In actual fact he was a friendly round-faced man with high cheek bones; Warnock, from films, knew his face as well as his own.

"You're lying behind Kaufmann at this stage. Let him set the pace—*your* pace. He won't mind. But save your energy for the Hungarian. You're pitting your fitness against Kaufmann; that's fixed in advance. You're playing chess with Horvath."

"Go on, Socrates," Colin shouted over his shoulder. Being with Jock was a tonic.

"Just don't bleddy well panic," came the grim voice. "Stick to Kaufmann like a bad smell."

They rolled up the bend, rhythmically, and prepared to enter the final straight. "The real danger comes now," said Jock sharply. "Catch me!" He bolted past Colin, thighs pumping, barrel chest stuck out: an uncouth missile.

"What the . . . !" Colin, taking up the challenge, kicked with all his strength. But with him "kick" was an inapt term; he wasn't capable of explosive bursts but ran in classic style, head back, legs eating the ground in huge strides.

The element of surprise had cost him a good five yards and there were less than a hundred to go. Jock was forty-five but had been a quarter-miler. Do what he might, he couldn't catch him. The burly figure with its scissoring thighs passed the line three yards in front of him.

They slowed and stopped; Jock was purple from the effort and his breath came like a death rattle. He clapped Colin on the shoulder: "Don't worry. Your kick's fine. I didna give you a chance." He turned aside to draw air into his congested lungs, walking off with short meandering steps as athletes do after their effort. His condition must have been good; in a few moments his heartbeat was almost back to normal, his breathing unforced.

"You sprung that one on me."

"Example is better than precept, as the dominie made me write out in copperplate when I was a shaver. —You see the danger: you can't let that Hungarian surprise you, not within a hundred yards of the tape. You're the wrong build to catch him again. Legs too long; you're a strider. Besides, he's quick on the run-in. You'll have to make your effort a fraction before his and let him push you home.

"But there's another danger: you mustn't hold back too long. Otherwise you'll lull yourself into a state where you can't take any initiative at all. Running's like anything else: you have to know when to hold yourself in and when to give." He filled his lungs with autumn air, in which the approaching cold mingled with the odour of shrivelling leaves. The wind conveyed that faint essence as well as the quarrelling of the rooks, the harsh jabber shrunk now to a gentle rumour.

Jock felt good now, in his element. He snuffed the air as eagerly as a fox before its earth. "Right then— do some more jogging if you like. I'm away to the gym—basketball. You specialists have a great time. Pampered like fighting cocks, you are. But I've my living to earn. See you."

Colin watched him put on his track suit, pick up his bicycle and ride off. Crafty old devil, he thought; pleased as Punch with his little trick. But who was he to complain? Jock had put him in a good humour. He felt strengthened and refreshed.

Professor Klaus Schuhmacher walked in the Botanic Gardens; it was half past four in the afternoon. The symmetrical beds, like the humped-up barrows of the Anglo-Saxon dead, lay clay-damp and brown, devastated of their flowers; the panes of the huge domed hothouse with its vines and bananas trees were blind, steamed over from the inside.

Decidedly, thought the professor, winter is on the way. The prospect pleased him: one could divide humanity into two groups, sun-lovers and shade-lovers, and he classed himself in the second category. The summer was a dangerously self-indulgent season, the sun an inexorable degenerator of the human stock, as the absorption of the Normans into the *far niente* of Sicily within three generations proved. The best time, the time of health, was typified for him by the frosty days of January when one's heels rang on the flagstones. That ring was a tuning fork for the mind; when it sounded thought took on vigour and harmony. The professor was obsessed with harmony, as a man is with something difficult to achieve.

There were a few late stragglers in the Gardens now, kicking through the fallen leaves Figures aimless in their movements or hurrying through, not exposing themselves to too strong a dose of nature.

He saw Colin Warnock come through the College Park gate, walking quickly. On the way home from Cherryvale, he guessed: the boy had no car, but took buses over town like his father, who had even spurned the Vice-Chancellor's Humber. "I've never spoiled myself in the past and I don't see why I should now," had been his attitude. Looking at Colin, Schuhmacher realised yet again how hard it must be for him to break free from the memory of that powerful man.

Coming up, Warnock said good day to him in German.

Oddly enough, he always used his mother's language with this man whom she despised.

Schuhmacher glanced at his travelling grip. "Training?" he enquired.

"Yes. Nothing strenuous though. I'm easing off before a big race."

Schuhmacher said, almost with a sigh: "How admirable to be able to subsume your aspirations in so simple a thing as a race. How obvious, how satisfying."

"You make it sound childish." Colin smiled; Jock's sanity was still strong in him.

Schuhmacher threw up his hands in horror. "Did I really give that impression?" His eyes shone with melancholy fanaticism. "I was actually envying you. You can justify yourself by beating a certain competitor or recording a certain time."

Warnock mused. "Is it serious though? I mean, devoting your life to covering a stretch of cinder track faster than the others?"

"My dear Colin," said the professor with great earnestness, "let no man presume to define what is serious and what is not. The wrestlers of antiquity were perhaps frivolous but they were celebrated by Pindar. The same is not true of writers of literary criticism." He smiled a sweet, secretive smile: very rueful, very Jewish. "And then, think of me in running kit! I have scrawny calves and my armpits are not pretty. —But believe me"—he resumed his natural seriousness without transition—"I do envy you. What you are doing is of vast importance. Every victory over oneself is."

"Ah. So you reduce it to the personal level: a victory over myself and therefore important only to me."

"What other victories are there?"

"Many, surely. Material victories. Let me put it this way: is it more important to set a world record or do what my father did?"

Schuhmacher sighed with something resembling impatience. "My dear boy, that is a foolish question. How can you compare the utilitarian with—well, with what I can only call the aesthetic? A great athletic performance does resemble art, if a thin-shanked fellow like me may speak about it. It purges and refreshes the human spirit—the spirit of those who watch, or read, or look, or listen." Holding both hands to his temples, he adjusted his spectacles, revealing the pale shiny hollow they had dug in the flesh of his nose.

He went on: "I was about to say there were no points of comparison between your father and you, but there is one: the growth of awareness. Robert Warnock, by the light of his own unaided intelligence, rose from being a simple agricultural expert in this remote province to the position of a practical prophet of the world's future. When he started life his preoccupations were no wider than his hundred acres at Crawfordsburn; but when that aeroplane crashed they covered the earth. Your physical arena is the track, but your field of awareness is much larger. Indeed it is the largest known to man, namely his own mind."

"It has its heroism too—is that what you mean?"

"Of course. Heroism is only an attitude. But it is attitude that determines achievement."

Colin reflected. "Father never had to work out his attitude to anything. He went straight ahead and acted. I wish I could be like that."

Schuhmacher smiled. "An unself-conscious man. He never ate of the tree of knowledge. And what strength with it! A force of nature." The shadow of the greenhouse, half-transparent, wavered on the trees. "You are going home now?" Colin nodded. "Let me come with you as far as the other gate. I am only out for a breath of air; one way is as good as another."

They walked up a little rise and then levelled off, the stark brick block of the Physics Department visible through the trees to their right. As they strolled Schuhmacher said: "He was a lucky man. The unself-conscious are lucky."

"He hated doubt. You know the story of the Gordian knot? It was the only historical anecdote he had any time for. But even it made him snort: 'Shame Alexander didn't put his good sense to better use!' he'd say."

"I remember the first time I got to know him. It was just after I came here, seventeen years ago. Of course we were acquainted before that, through your mother's family; but we didn't really become familiar until one famous day in University Road. We were crossing the street together, going to Queen's Elms, I remember, when a car went out of control and mounted the pavement beside us. A beggar pulled Robert out of the way; probably saved his life. Then the man touched his cap and held out his hand for money. Robert refused on the grounds that the state provided for the unemployed." He gave a soundless laugh.

Warnock squirmed. How many times had he not been shamed as a child when some such story got into the press? His class mates would be full of jocular admiration: "Your oul fella's a real character!" they would say. But there was no mistaking the sly hostility under it. And Colin felt the need to repudiate this character, who happened to be his father. It rose in him now: how like the old bugger to make pure principle appear wilful cruelty and not care a damn if he did!

"I thought him the most appalling bear I had ever met," Schuhmacher was saying. "But then we got into conversation and in half an hour I considered myself privileged to know him."

They reached the freakish little brick gate lodge with its Gothic-looking clock. "Well, I must leave you here. I turn right."

"*Auf Wiedersehen.*"

"*Auf Wiedersehen*. Don't doubt yourself, Colin, just because you are your father's son. You are no Richard Cromwell."

The house in Balmoral Avenue was as silent and tomb-like as an exclusive club. Indeed a club was what it most resembled, he thought as he sat at table, alone, in the dark dining room. It had been his for two years now; but he had not become master of it, or of the comfortable income left in trust for him, until his coming of age a month ago. Amused, he said to himself: "I am a property owner." There was the farm in North Down, let out to a good tenant, along with two other pieces of land he had never heard about until the reading of the will; they had been left to Robert by an admirer. There were also the moderate holdings in gilt-edged stock, the surprising ten thousand pounds in accident insurance, and this house.

This club with no members. From outside it was an ordinary brick and slate villa, with the frowning look that houses take on in a rainy country; inside there was a profusion of sombre wood panelling, deep-polished wood-block flooring and a murky window in stained glass on the landing half way up the stairs.

The furniture was mahogany, solid as the rock of Gibraltar; the curtains bottle-green velvet, touched with the yellowing patina of age. Put your face to them and you were overpowered by an aroma of dust—not the gross deposit of an unswept house, but that quintessential dust that settles on the lives and dwelling places of the mercantile bourgeoisie of provincial cities. He was used to the smell and did not dislike it.

Mrs McArdle, the middle-aged housekeeper he had inherited from his father, cleared his dinner plate and brought his pudding. She was as silent as the house itself and had perhaps been chosen for that reason. She still called him Mr Colin.

Looking up from his plate, his saw on the wall opposite him

47

one of those black ebony heads in low relief which Robert had brought back from that famous Kenya expedition years before he was born. The house was full of souvenirs of it: camel-skin briefcases with decorative motifs made up of leather thongs, leopard-skin rugs, a crudely carved elephant's tusk, all old and worn now. The rugs, with their massive heads and merciless eyes, had scared him as a child, but by now they had merged into the shabby gentility of the house.

The Kikuyu shield with crossed spears that greeted you when you stepped into the chilly hall—that was natural here too, as were the rows of much-annotated books in the study and the cupboards bulging with papers that some future biographer would certainly want to investigate; Colin himself had not had the courage to look into them.

In the study after coffee, he pulled a slim green volume at random from the overflowing shelves. As chance would have it, it was his father's study *The Physique and Health Of The Kikuyu Tribe of Kenya*. Dry-as-dust stuff on the surface, with its tables showing the average height and development of African children under different dietary conditions, plus hieroglyphs on soil chemistry. A mere academic treatise, one of the many that saw the light in 1926; but it had brought together two things which had, incredibly, never been linked before: the composition of the soil and the health of the people whom it feeds. Colin flicked over the pages to the conclusion, printed in heavy black lettering:

". . . The problem, therefore, concerns not only the public health authorities but also those in charge of agriculture. The mineral content of the soil determines the health and well-being of those who live from it."

Robert had brought home from Kenya, along with his assorted skins and shields, the distinction of having uncovered a great truism.

Colin suddenly thought: I have no more identity than one of those ebony heads. His pusillanimous behaviour with Beth proved it. He blushed for himself: why was it that some paralysing blight touched him when he tried to act as ordinary people did?

But not on the track . . . No doubt about it: if he wanted to make something of himself it would have to be there. Not in Jock's unthinking way, for which he had a sudden pang of nostalgia. That paradise was lost to him; he could never be the man Jock wanted him to be, at least not in the way Jock wanted it. He was Schuhmacher's man; he had eaten of the tree of knowledge.

But success was not beyond him; he was a Schuhmacher whose field of activity had been transposed by sleight of hand into Jock's. His task was to do better there than the native-born.

He felt oddly lighter at shouldering his eternal burden of self-consciousness. And Schuhmacher was right: he *was* no Richard Cromwell. There was physical strength inside him and somewhere, locked inside that, a moral strength that might well be enough to give him the things he longed for.

His problem was one of realisation. He had to tap the resource he felt inside, convert that hidden reserve into something as prosaic as foot-pounds per second. It was as easy, and as difficult, as that.

VI

The dressing room at Santry stadium in Dublin. A bare unremarkable place with distempered walls and deal flooring. Creepers of clothing trailing from hooks. The young men who had discarded them were sitting in their track suits, brooding and subdued; the explosion of talk and laughter, the flood of exultation and excuse would come later.

Occasionally someone would squeak across the room on spikes and make his way out into the cold autumnal day. A loudspeaker relayed instructions and information, but nobody was really listening: they all knew their places on the card.

The distinctive thing was the smell, an intoxicating whiff of sweet and acrid composed of man-odour (the warm humours of shirt and undervest), dusty wood, camphor rub, towelling and urinal-stench. An alarming cocktail when you first encountered it, but Colin was familiar with it by now. He sat putting his spikes on: they smelt of hardened leather, ingrained cinders, crushed grass-blades.

Hunter and Foley were with him; they had only local opposition and would win. His own opponents were not far away, Kaufmann and Horvath, each accompanied by his trainer. They had come on the same plane and now found themselves staying at the same hotel, drawn together as foreigners but unable to forget that they were rivals too; they hardly spoke to one another.

Jock had come to Dublin too, but wasn't with his athletes; he scorned the pampering of modern runners and refused to act as a buffer between them and the real world. "For Christ's sake look after yersels, ye're big and ugly enough" was his motto.

He was out there somewhere, in the crowd.

A voice was whispering in Colin's ear: "I'm on in ten minutes": Foley. He moved off with downcast eyes, making for the underground passage. Two others got nervously to their feet; they were in the same race and followed him as though they feared he might steal a march by being first in the field.

"Good luck, Brendan. And up King Billy!" Hunter called, but without conviction. His event was only two places down from Foley's.

Minutes passed. The first returning competitors came in: sprinters who had just run the two-twenty. "Who won, Harry?" Hunter asked one of them, a ginger-haired youth.

"Kevin here. As bloody usual."

"What was the time?"

"Twenty-one point five or something. —I got a bloody awful start."

"Christ, I'd fancy myself at that rate. Ireland just can't produce a sprinter."

"Thanks, mac. How about you—broken fifty yet?"

Kaufmann was standing up to strip: a real athlete, thought Colin with a pang: bigger-boned, more heavily muscled than I am. But what lightness just the same!

Beside him Horvath was almost a comic figure; six inches shorter, receding hair, his whole body covered in a black pelt: a powerful, crafty ancestor of man. More like a boxer than a middle distance runner. Still, one of the five fastest men in the world. Broken four minutes many times.

Colin was now changed; all three of them were standing-up, track-suited, anonymous blue teddy bears. He went over to them.

"*Darf ich mich vorstellen* . . . ?" He introduced himself. Polite astonishment that he spoke German, feigned surprise at his identity (feigned because their trainers had been feeding them with his performances for days past; they knew he was Ireland's white hope, a wonder boy: some day they might seriously have to reckon with him).

Horvath smiled at him, a smile of surprising gentleness. His cheekbones were high, his eyes slightly slanting: a true Magyar. He spoke telegraphese German: "This track—you like—very fast—yes?"

"Yes," said Warnock.

"World records made here—often—we do good time—no?"

The word *record* made Colin suddenly nervous. The muscle wall of his abdomen tightened a fraction, like a belt.

"We have never run here before," Kaufmann was saying in a pleasant voice. "The stadium is small, but I like it." His hair was blond and floppy, his face handsome in a soft way, not really in keeping with the taut-muscled frame. As with so many athletes, head and body didn't quite seem to belong together.

"I daresay it is a bit small compared with some of the places you have in Germany. But we're rather proud of it here; it's our first."

Kaufmann hastened to apologise; one felt he was also apologising for being a German, for the Nazis, for everything. Colin felt a wave of sympathy for him.

"Did you fly?"

"Yes. Yesterday afternoon. I had hoped to see a little of the country from the plane—they say it's beautiful—but there was cloud."

Horvath laughed. "Much rain here—no?"

"Much rain yes," said Colin. "But the track's in good shape."

A knot of athletes came in, chop-fallen and breathless. It was the half-milers, Foley among them. He was breathing harshly, had a fleck of foam on his upper lip. Each cheek-bone wore a circle of bright red.

"Did you do it?" called Hunter.

"Aye. Under one forty-nine. My best." He smiled a tired, secretive smile.

"Saving it up for the big day, eh? Off you go then, for a wash and confession." Hunter stood up, yawned nervously and pounded his chest. "Right, young hopefuls. Come and get beaten."

He walked off.

The three milers fell silent. The time for talk was over; from now they were dedicated to the task of humiliating each other.

They could be friends again later. They turned their backs on each other.

Steam hissed from the showers next door. One of the eight-eighty men passed, bathing Colin in pungent sweat-smell. He let himself down on the wooden bench and leaned on the arrested cascade of his clothes. A gentle paralysis had overcome him, leaving him empty of desire or will. He floated away in a kind of dream, a dream through which tiny fingers of anxiety probed, riding on the anonymous words from the loudspeaker. The anxiety was held in a suspension, like powder in a liquid, colouring everything but not yet ready to fall to the bottom and be identified.

Minutes passed.

At last it was time to go. The three rose in a body and went to the passage. Three other runners, the make-weights, followed.

They walked out on to the cinder track. This was the organised chaos of an athletics meeting; there was no applause. It wasn't like the roar that Hunter drank in when the national rugby team ran out, passing the bright orange ball. People were too busy watching the pole vault or the boys' steeplechase or the ladies' discus. You just walked stiffly across the track into the oval green island inside.

All six separated, to warm up in some private corner. Colin wandered over to a couple of other Queen's athletes who were sitting moodily on a bench, picking divots from their spikes.

A steward in a white coat bustled across officiously to check who he was, what was his business. His identity determined, he walked over to the cinders and tested them as a swimmer takes the temperature of the water. Kaufmann and Horvath were doing the same, but more assiduously: the track was new to them.

The day was cold, with a remnant of sunshine and a small

biting wind: he must keep moving. A ripple of applause, for a shot-putt performance. Over sixty feet, a good one. Colin loosened up on the spot, lifting his knees high, pretending to sprint. His blood began to circulate.

A sudden bang; the crowd's slow roar rose in pitch. Colin looked and saw the eight four-forty men rise from their blocks in a staggered line and surge round the bend like power boats breasting an invisible sea. Hunter had drawn the outside lane and couldn't see what his opponents were doing; his great rangy body was a target for them. He was ahead at the furlong but it was too early to say. They swept past where Warnock was jerking up and down like a demented sea-anemone, reduced to invertebrate status by his track suit. They came in a flurry of speed and effort, their cheeks blowing in and out. Colin, suddenly exhilarated, willed Hunter to win.

And win he did, coming out of the top bend in the lead and surging up the final stretch with one shoulder raised, a rugby three-quarter running in from the twenty-five with no one to lay a finger on him. The time: forty-eight. Reasonable.

Warnock felt absurdly happy. He thought: Foley first, then Hunter. My turn next. Well, he would do it. His nerves fell away. He thought momentarily of his father and felt the equal of him; he was going to run.

There was a women's hurdles before the mile. The girls were at the start now, hammering in their blocks. A couple were practising starts, buttocks in the air. Thank God Beth only played tennis, thought Warnock ungenerously. He finished his jogging, went through a short routine of arm jerks and breathed deeply, in and out, thirty times. In the middle of this performance the girls were given the gun and immediately called back with a second shot. One had broken too early; she came back, tossing her head.

Another bang, muscular female thighs thrashed, a couple of

hurdles toppled and it was over. The girl who had jumped the gun won; she pranced up and down with joy. The others stood with hands on hips, faintly censorious, getting their breath back. The loudspeaker crashed in with the result and time, then went on: "Next event: men's invitation mile. Competitors as follows. Number one: James Mulcahy of Donore Harriers. Number two . . ."

This, then, was the test.

He was second from the inside, on Mulcahy's right: Mulcahy a nonentity, but one who might affect the result by setting a bad pace or interfering with a more fancied runner at a vital moment . . . Mulcahy stood staring morosely at the ground.

Outside Colin: Horvath. Giving all and sundry a reassuring smile. Then another unknown, Ignatius Flynn of Clonliffe. Then Kaufmann, standing easily, looking confident. On the outside Drew Dickson of East Down: an old campaigner, balder than Horvath, a cross-country runner with the cross-countryman's habit of chewing gum as he ran; his stubbly jaws were moving now.

"Take your marks!"

They emptied their heads of all save running and projected their corporate will forward. In each of the six minds silence fell, though the crowd was bellowing hysterically: this was what most of them had come for.

"SE-E-ET-T!"

A deep, indrawn breath, a reaching forward of six bodies, lasting perhaps a second: a second of intolerable strain which yet existed in another world, a world with misty outlines and monochrome horizons, the world of the competing athlete whose blood has been drawn off from the head to nourish the legs and haunches.

Crack. They lunged forward into a domain where everything happened very fast and with hieratic slowness at the same time. A region too where the tension of the start was blown away by a great wind and you were left with none but physical preoccupations: the thickening of saliva, the soaring of breathing rate and heartbeat, the convulsive holding-in of limbs aching to expend themselves in one oblivion-bringing spurt.

Mulcahy had jumped into the lead and trailed the others behind him by an invisible cord. Horvath, second, bowling along like a sailor. Colin on his heels, his brooding face held downwards, his long stride making him appear to float. Then Flynn and Dickson, moving with ill-concealed embarrassment, like other ranks being served by their officers on Christmas Day. Last, Kaufmann, running with the elastic stride that had brought him world records at this distance and at fifteen hundred metres until an iron man from the Antipodes had clipped fractions of a second off them.

For the next two laps nothing changed. They forged steadily round the track, lulled by a common rhythm like marching soldiers. Their eyes were glazed, apparently in reverie.

But the reverie was phoney. The higher levels of consciousness had been switched off, saving the supply of concentration for more basic things; but in all six an alert caveman cunning was awake; they stalked each other like animals. There was a voluptuous pleasure in this double state.

Half way through the third lap they awoke. Mulcahy, who had set a faster pace than he could maintain in a queer determination not to be written off by these international stars, was wavering. You could see his will-power crumble with each step; he was tottering on his feet.

The sight filled Colin with alarm. A crisis! Something must be done. The temptation to assert his own superiority, to glide past the beaten man and show the field an insolent pair of heels, was intense. He might even have yielded to it but for

Horvath, running in front of him. He had an almost physical sense that the Hungarian was deliberately holding back, refusing to make a move.

But that very reluctance was switching the burden of responsibility to *him*! He was in torment. His mind told him: don't be a fool, don't make a break, be patient. But his body clamoured for the sudden thrilling rush, the quasi-erotic liberation. My God, I'm cracking, he cried inwardly, I'm going to break, I just can't help myself!

With a wave of relief he heard a faster tempo of footsteps behind him and Ignatius Flynn bolted past like a rabbit and led them all in a helter-skelter dash round the rest of the lap. Colin was full of relief and exultation: what a fool he'd been to think *he* was the only one feeling the pressure!

They all lengthened their strides and followed Flynn, a scrawny young man with brilliantined hair and a pointed nose; there was something lazily cruel about them, like cats about to pounce on a mouse. They knew that Flynn couldn't last.

Sure enough, the strident clangour of the bell re-established natural order. It drove its barbed message into Flynn's head: bravely as you've struggled, it said, the ordeal isn't over. In fact the worst is yet to come. Appalling prospect: suddenly he was finished, his lungs could no longer bring enough oxygen to his flailing limbs. He fell back.

Another crisis, another alarm: who was going to be fool enough to take the lead now, with less than four hundred to go? Horvath was still refusing and there was nothing to hope for from the third of the rabbits, the gum-chewing Dickson, who was by now blowing heavily.

Astonishingly, the problem was solved. Helmut Kaufmann, disdainful of this ignoble loitering, sailed round the outside of the bunch and turned into the second-last bend, moving with supple strength.

Horvath and Warnock stayed at his shoulder, setting their feet in the very marks of his. The outsiders dropped behind, out of the race now. It was to be the three-man battle the crowd had waited for.

With every stride they drew nearer to the point of true crisis, the moment when their trinity of wills would coalesce, ignite and explode the race into some dire new shape. Colin felt another devil of panic stir in him. He had never experienced this before, his senses cried out for what he was used to, the triumphant run-in free from opposition. A tempest of impatience shook him: Now! Now! It was far too early, there was still half a lap to go, but Horvath was there in front of him, and what had Jock said? Surprise him, make your break before him at all costs.

He broke. And then the script started to go wrong. The Hungarian, infected by the same insanity as himself, bounded forward at the precise moment that Colin reached his shoulder. They ran side by side, Colin losing yards on the outside of the bend. They passed Kaufmann; the crowd bayed "Warnock! Warnock!" with inarticulate intensity.

Colin's mind was drenched with violence; he could have done murder. He hated Horvath, he was determined to humiliate him. Faster! Faster! he raged to himself. They swung round the final bend neck and neck. Horvath was cursing himself inwardly:he was mad, mad! But it was too late. He had to fight it out now, on this ground, whatever the outcome. He dared not relax his battle-urge so close to the finish.

Colin summoned all his resources for a last effort. With stupefaction and despair he realised that it wasn't going to come. He had nothing left. The Hungarian slowly drew away from him.

Hunching his shoulders, driving his head like a wedge into the space between them, he sawed his arms back and forth and clenched his fists inches from his face, trying to force himself into the rhythm of a sprint. But it was no good. I'm exhausted! he realised. I'm going to faint! His body was only just capable of staying upright; its own momentum carried it along.

Yet paradoxically he felt that he had not really given everything. Deep down, untouched, there was a final spring of energy he had not been able to tap. The conviction drove him to further furious efforts, but in vain. Something in him was refusing service. He was like a rugby player who funks a tackle, not from lack of mental resolution but because his body draws back from it. His body had drawn back from this final test.

He half-saw Kaufmann sweep past him, great runner that he was. In a trice the German was on terms with Horvath, they battled it out shortly, but it was a foregone conclusion. The Hungarian had made his effort too soon and lost by five yards.

Colin staggered past the line a further ten away. He could see a television camera on the roof of the stand panning round, following Kaufmann. This was the supreme humiliation. He brushed his would-be helpers aside and walked blindly back to the changing room.

Chapter 2

I

Warnock was consumed with rage and impatience. He longed to break the mould of his life without really knowing how. Finally, he bought a car.

It was the hard-top model of a famous racing make, a long, gleaming missile with a compartment for driver and passenger that looked like an aeroplane cockpit.

Now he was faced with the problem of a driving licence. He hired an instructor for six hours a day and memorised the code in the evenings. A week later he announced "I must be tested immediately," hardly recognising himself in this wilful young man who insisted on having his own way. He passed without trouble.

Then his aggressiveness slackened. He found himself with nothing to do. "I'd better go back to lectures," he told himself; he had not appeared at Queen's since the fiasco, shrinking from the presence of people who knew him, people who had read the Sunday headlines: WARNOCK FAILS. WONDER BOY FLOPS.

He had spent a couple of days mooning around Dublin, a city he did not particularly like, looking at the Book of Kells in the library of Trinity College, inspecting Joyce's Martello tower at Sandycove and the Impressionist pictures in the National Gallery of Ireland. In Davy Byrne's he suffered some of that sparkling Irish pub conversation which has so high a reputation in the outside world. At last impatience closed the wound and he rushed home to buy his car.

So now it was lectures again. It would have to come to that, he knew, but he was embarrassed at the thought of meeting Beth. By some odd logic the loss of the race obliged him to make a move where she was concerned; he owed it to her. Of course he wanted it himself, but he was afraid of what he wanted.

He made his appearance the following morning at Schuhmacher's Friday lecture. The professor raised his eyebrows a fraction and nodded to him before beginning to speak. Warnock sat through the performance rigidly, taking an occasional note. His eyes avoided Beth, almost brutally.

Only as they were all filing out of the room did he shoulder his way across to her and fling out between clenched teeth: "Come for a drive with me tomorrow."

Her face was tinged with pink along the line of the cheek-bones. For a moment he thought she was going to spit his graceless invitation back in his face, but she merely said "All right" in a low voice. She had won a round; that was enough to stifle her annoyance.

They arranged to meet at ten o'clock the following morning.

II

He had made no other alteration in his life. The house, with its faded velvet and old leather, was a shrine; he could change nothing in it without changing all, and was far from ready for that. So it was after the usual Saturday breakfast in the dark dining room that he slammed the door behind him, stepped into the little tourer and roared off down the Lisburn Road. It was a cheerless morning with a steady drip from the roof-eaves. A watery sun shone whitely through the blanket of cloudy damp that enveloped the city. There was no wind; the purr of his exhaust ricocheted heavily from the house fronts.

He turned right at Windsor Avenue and stopped outside Beth's house, with the skeletal hedge of the tennis club to his right. No play today; the courts were dark red and soaking. He sounded the high-pitched horn.

She came down in a moment, dressed in a chunky purple overcoat with a broad collar that buttoned up in front of the chin. The colour showed off her hair breath-takingly; it flowed like jet-black liquid against the bulky material. But it made her look pale too and brought out the uneasiness in her eyes.

They were too embarrassed to say much at first. Colin thought: the car will do the trick. He swung it out into the Malone Road with a flourish. Then left along Stranmillis, and a plunge down a steep street of red brick houses on to the Lagan embankment. From there they debouched on to a crowded artery overlooking a cemetery and a golf course, twin monuments of suburbia, and dawdled south in heavy traffic until the semi-detached villas petered out. After that he was able to give the car its head, watching Beth's exhilaration from the corner of his eye.

They forged south through frowning villages where women trailed shopping baskets and men stood at windy corners, towards the mountain country of Mourne. As they drove the sky lifted and dampness drained out of the air; but it was still a chill autumn day. The sky remained grey and there were puddles in the roadside ditches.

"I didn't even know you had a car," Beth finally said.

"I didn't till a week ago."

"Somehow I don't associate you with driving. I mean,

you're not one of the motor sport gang, with leather gloves and the latest Porsche. Or an old-car fancier with a ginger beard, baggy cords and a 1929 Rolls-Royce painted yellow."

"I'm not very fashionable."

She risked it. "You're too nice for that." Colin's hands shook on the wheel but he hadn't the courage to smile at her. As for Beth, she thought, tensely: I'm having to make all the running. "Actually I like the car," she added feebly.

Colin, called upon to demonstrate it, swept past a lorry on a short straight. Another sports car suddenly appeared at the next corner, flying towards him, devouring the road. He pressed his foot down blindly and contrived to slide into the gap between lorry and car; through his panic he had a startled glimpse of the driver's horrified face.

When he was able to look at Beth he saw that her hands were still clasped together; the knuckles were white. His spirits fell. There was a complicated system of barricades between them; when he had negotiated one there was always another waiting for him.

They drove into Newcastle, a spick-and-span seaside town with amusements arcades, ice cream parlours and street signs in bold lettering. There were few people around at this time of year, and on the artificial lake by the bridge the blue rowing boats were tied together in a line and fastened to a little man-made island. There was something desolate about them.

"It's strange," Beth said, "but I've never been here before. We always went to Portrush."

"We came here often. It used to have such charm, but now it's being developed."

They had fetched up looking through a grimy cement arch at the huge sweep of the Mourne Mountains; they had had them in their sights for the past ten miles but now, close up, their sheer size was overwhelming; they crushed the narrow ribbon of the town.

Beth's eyes took in the great domed summits, which rose nearly three thousand feet in a single bound, and the scree-scarred lower slopes, shaggy with trees. What a magnificent domain it was, half-wild, half-domesticated, a paradise of trees, gorse and bracken. But at sea level it had been devastated. The whole area in front of them had been turned into a car park, with asphalt, concrete and the soggy remains of the summer's trippers. A little further away the natural meadow had been fenced in to make a football pitch.

"I used to play there when I was a child," said Colin. "But they'd started even then. It drove my father wild. He kept writing to the papers, but it did no good."

They went on down the coast to the village of Annalong; the twin basins of its tiny harbour were crammed with fishing boats and men in rubber boots walked in and out of the public house. An unspoiled place, this: no beach to lure the tourist. They walked on the quay for a quarter of an hour with their collars drawn up round their faces, then climbed back into the car and returned to Newcastle to have lunch in the big red hotel beside the golf course. Colin felt a tremor of guilt as they walked in; the memory of his father's frugality rebuked him. Signing the cheque for the car had been a struggle.

They were the only customers, apart from a red-faced priest who was clearly no stranger either to the hotel of the links. He called the waiters by their Christian names and waded into his food. Colin and Beth ate quietly; the same thought had come into their heads: these people think we're honeymooners. They left quickly after coffee.

"Where to now?" said Colin.

"Can we stay close to the mountains? I've never seen them before, remember."

He drove her up to the neat village of Bryansford. To begin

with the road ran between over-arching trees. The hedges were choked with leaves, wet and rotting; an aroma of decomposition—the warm, pregnant decomposition of autumn—blew in through the side windows. It was melancholy and exciting at the same time. They felt themselves caught up in a great natural process; speech would be an impertinence. Even the low hum of the engine was an embarrassment.

They emerged from under the trees to find themselves mounting a glen-like valley with a salmon stream brawling over granite boulders far down to the left. Beyond that rose a mountain covered with a sheep's pelt of trees and bushes; some had been ravaged red by autumn, but there was among them a stiffening of evergreens with blackened emerald spines, clustered together in small plantations or standing alone. "It's beautiful!" Beth cried, her eyes shining. Thank God for nature, thought Colin.

In front of them were ragged hills, bracken above, small stony fields below, squatting decorously behind iron gates mounted on fat stone gateposts, bright with new whitewash.

Colin drove in a trance he was afraid to break. They purred along the switchback roads, slowing for a cart drawn by a horse with hairy hooves, or stopped altogether by a herd of pigs wallowing across. On the left there was a russet hill with skimpy fields climbing to the limit of cultivable earth. Its ridge had the shape of one of the pigs' backs, and a single line of trees grew along it, like bristles.

When they were opposite a two-headed mountain—a perfectly symmetrical double cone—Beth turned to him. "Colin, let's . . ."

He needed no further invitation. They stopped the car, climbed the fence into a field and ran towards the mountain. The ground was soaking but they didn't care, running on and on, cavorting like rabbits in springtime, bounding off in great irregular loops. Colin sprinted, his coat-tails flying.

"It's wonderful, wonderful!" panted Beth.

"Let's go on, into the hollow there."

"Lead the way."

A scrap of morning mist lay in the depression before them, swathing the grass in wispy grey, rising to the very door of a farm house that stood without a sign of life behind a high square rampart of privet hedge. There was a horse, standing perfectly still, his hooves covered to the fetlocks by the clinging vapour.

Suddenly he expelled his breath in twin vapour trials and cantered off like a ghost, his feet touching no ground. The silent spell was broken. Colin looked at Beth and knew he loved her, exclusively, sickeningly, with a young man's love. He wanted to do something desperate and beautiful, take her into his own body perhaps.

Perhaps, in a moment, he would have made his move; but Beth was impatient and flung away from him shouting,"What's the name of that damned mountain anyway?"

"I don't know."

"Call yourself a County Down man!"

He knew perfectly well, but couldn't bring himself to say it. It was called the Cock and Hen mountain.

They went dispiritedly back to the car, Beth throwing out her legs as she walked. What's wrong with me? she brooded. Am I a leper or something?

Warnock was paralysed. He loved her but hardly dared think of what love implied. In the first place he was so ignorant of it; perhaps he would be impotent, unable to play man's part at all. And even if not, what might it all lead to? Where would it leave his running: could running and Beth be reconciled? He longed to touch her, to gain at least temporary relief. But he didn't dare.

The heart had fallen out of the day for them. They could have gone further but Beth vetoed it. Instead they made for the main Dublin-Belfast road, driving in silence through the deserted countryside. Everything was dank with the year's end; here and there black smoke billowed from a pyre of withered leaves. In some places a farmer was doing his autumn ploughing, riding high on an orange tractor, the curved blades turning up peat-brown earth full of stubble-stalks, huge wriggling worms, abandoned nests of field mice like little piles of hay chewed small. A seeping melancholy drenched the landscape.

By the time they reached the market town of Dromore the lights were lit and shining a ghastly yellow. Beth was huddled up in her purple coat, sunk into herself. Colin couldn't find a word to say.

Lisburn passed, and with it the tentacles of the city began. They drove past villas standing among wet trees, red estates with forests of television aerials, roadhouses with neon signs reading: Abandon hope, all ye who enter here.

At last the car turned into Windsor Avenue. They got out under the beech tree in the garden of her house and stood there, miserable and cold. All the joy had drained out of the world. Colin would have crawled anonymously away, giving up for good, but when he looked at Beth he saw such mute suffering in her face that he forgot everything and held out his arms to her. They kissed mutely, in relief more than anything else.

They went inside and made fumbling, anguished love on Beth's settee; then, tired but keyed up at the same time, drove to the roadhouse with the most garish sign for dinner. That night they slept together in the small bedroom with the chintz curtains.

III

What was to be done about Jock? Warnock kept well away from Cherryvale and the gym; he feared the Scotsman's tongue. But he couldn't leave him in the dark like this. Something would have to be done. So he wrote a letter.

> Dear Jock,
>   I've decided to give up training for the winter. What's the point in keeping fit when the first athletics meeting is in May?
>   To tell you the truth, I need a rest from running. It's rather taken over my life. I want to grow fat for a while!
>   My regards to your wife and children.
>   Colin Warnock

Disingenuous, and also pointless: he didn't even mention the issue of the cross country season, which was just about to begin. He ran at number one for Queen's and knew he would be sorely missed. So he expected a wrathful reply. But none came and in a strange way he was disappointed.

He was right about growing fat. His weight gradually crept up. "Bah," said Beth when he looked mildly concerned, "you're happy, that's all. —Well, aren't you?"

He was. In her arms he found the release into strength and confidence that, *pace* Schuhmacher, Nietzsche experienced with the lightning flash. He soon set aside the queasy embarrassment of virginity and became an assured lover, alternating between the tender and the demonic, giving himself up to the dictates of the moment. As for Beth, his male strength gave her the self-forgetfulness she craved and lowered the emotional pressure under which she lived. Her instinct about him, she reflected triumphantly, had been right.

But Warnock spent no more nights at her flat; it wasn't fair to her. "You're a girl, you have more to lose," he said. "Unless we got married . . . Why don't we, Beth?"

"I'm a minor. I'd have to have Daddy's consent."

"Ring up and ask him then."

She tossed her head. "You have no conception of what it's like in a country town. Things have to be done properly."

"You don't mean that the Czar of Limavady is susceptible to public opinion?"

She put her hand over his mouth; he kissed it. "Be serious, you mutt. He has his position to think about. I shall have to invite you down for Christmas—as a friend, naturally. You'll drink with his cronies and be sized up. The next step would normally be for you to invite *me* to *your* parents'. But that's not possible so I don't know what the next step is. But it's a slow process, I can tell you."

"What if . . . if we get careless?"

She frowned. "We don't. We can't afford to."

"All right. But let's get secretly engaged. I have a yearning to go to a jeweller's and spend a great deal of money on a ring."

"No! No!" She flung herself on him, shaking him by the shoulders. "Observe decorum. German barbarian!" They ended on the carpet, making love.

They never went to his house. Beth had seen the outside of it often enough but refused to go inside. "What a tomb!" she said. "I don't know why you go on living in it."

"It's a perfectly ordinary house!" he retorted. "The entire Ulster bourgeoisie inhabits the like."

"No it doesn't. Some of them live in brick towers with glass all down one side. Some live in tasteful villas on suburban estates. *I* live in a converted Georgian farmhouse full of flowers. So there."

"Indeed. Well, let me tell you, madam, that my house is sensitive and resents criticism. You shall never darken its doors."

"Don't want to. Sucks to you." So she never entered the house in Balmoral Avenue.

They attended lectures in the usual way, making no attempt to sit together; but everybody knew something was going on. Neither of them had any taste for circular arguments about literature over bad coffee in the Union, so they didn't go there. When classes were over Colin would take Beth away in the car, discreetly parked behind the university in Rugby Avenue.

They came to identify the countryside with their happiness. Both were confirmed walkers in any case, Colin from his natural athleticism which needed an outlet now, Beth from old habit: she knew every mountain in Donegal.

They went back to the Mournes, to climb the trapezium of Binnian with its castellated crowns; but only once, when the weather forecast was unambiguous. At that season the light lasted only till four o'clock, and then who knew what rain storm or sudden mist might not come down?

From the mountain's high windy shoulder they looked down on the Silent Valley reservoir, a broad gash in the rock containing a man-made lake, wedge-shaped like a primitive axe head. The walls of the surrounding mountains were deep grey shading into black, veined and spotted by crystals of granite. High up, under the conical hat of one of the peaks, a silver lake glinted like a horizontal mirror; a quicksilver torrent left it to tumble down into the reservoir hundreds of feet below.

They were standing on the extreme end of a horseshoe of peaks that swung round one central slab. The opposite end was the huge mass of Donard. Between it and them was another valley, with the rocky bed of a stream that flowed down to the sea at Annalong. All around them was utter silence; not a bird nor an animal to break it. Peace seeped into them like some beneficent draught.

At other times they went to the Antrim coast, or to Slieve Gullion, crouching secretively among the shaggy fields of South Armagh. But usually they did no more than drive out beyond the urban sprawl and walk along a country road or across the fields.

It was November and the landscape was sacked by autumn. All the soil's produce had been brought in; the few birds that remained in these latitudes perched forlornly on the telegraph wires, their feathers blown awry, or stepped out delicately where the tractor had passed, picking about the sticky upturned glebe for whatever living thing the plough might reveal: a sickly white grub or a purple worm.

The hawthorn hedges were now no more than a knotted tangle of twigs, like thin arthritic fingers. The afternoons were chill and keen, but every now and then the Irish autumn made a free gift of a sunny day that threw a half-cheerful half-melancholy light on the fields and took the bone from the wind. Then the old intoxication would rise from the land: a powerful, dizzying perfume that was at its strongest in summer when to go out among the growing oats and potatoes was to have you mind confused and muddled by a sweet unreality, insubstantial as the blue hills floating on the distant heat haze. It was in Warnock's experience a quality peculiar to Ireland, and had to do with the humidity that hung over the country all year round. It was productive of a delightful lethargy, a giddiness of the spirit that Beth and he felt again on this last bright day of the year. The only antidote was to emigrate to some place where the sun was king.

But they had no intention of emigrating. They ambled through the bare fields, their feet wet by a flax dam, with its eloquent stink and brimming, brown-glinting water.

One day they came on a corrugated-iron barn standing on

wooden stakes. Joyfully they prised open the ramshackle door and squeezed in, clambering up on to the dessicated hay. There, bathed in the insipid aroma, their hair full of stalks, they made love for half the afternoon until the gathering dark told them it was time to go.

They stumbled across the fields to the car, arms entwined, yawning and laughing at each other.

IV

One Sunday Beth had to entertain a Derry friend of her mother's. Colin, unable to sit at home alone, went walking on the embankment. The sky was overcast but there was no sign of rain; the wind was driving the clouds tumultuously and blowing up irregular ripples here and there on the surface of the river. He was striding out, face against the wind, by the green-painted railings at the water side.

Ahead of him, a pair of figures emerged from the neat estate to the left. They crossed the roadway and came towards him: a dumpy, middle-aged woman in a royal blue coat and a pink hat from which grew a variety of plastic fruits and a stoutish, eminently respectable man in a dove-grey crombie coat with a bowler clamped decisively on his bullet head. Too late, he realised it was Mr and Mrs Jock.

Before he had time to recover from his confusion they had come up to him and the bowler had been doffed, ceremoniously and with a hint of mockery. Warnock was in a state of panic: this was a totally different Jock from the one he knew! If he had met him on the track, humanised by his brawny calves, he might have slipped into the old cheeky familiarity—but how could one be familiar with such an apparition?

"Ethel, permit me to introduce Mr Warnock. Mr *Colin* Warnock." The formality was barbed; he had the advantage and didn't intend to lose it.

"Pleased to meet you, Mrs Campbell."

"My husband has told me about you. You're Robert Warnock's son, aren't you? And a runner like my Jock used to be—"

"Aye," Jock broke in. His wife, being one of those women whom nervousness makes voluble, was about to say something more when he went on: "Colin laddie."

"Yes?"

"Did you see the Pink last night?"

"No. To tell you the truth, I'm a bit out of touch."

"The Harriers were beaten into third place at Lurgan. East Antrim won."

Colin swallowed. "Didn't they run well or something?"

"We packed five men into the first twenty places. But you know as well as I do that we haven't a decent number six. I tried McKillen but he could do nae better than thirty-ninth. East Antrim beat us easy. Even Duncairn got their noses in front o' us—by a single point." He sighed. "That's how it's goin' to be for the rest o' the season."

"You can't win all the time," Mrs Campbell observed with a strained laugh. "Life's full of ups and downs."

"You're perfectly right, Ethel," said Jock solemnly.

"Well, there's no point in crying over it," Warnock rejoined, suddenly defiant. "I say good luck to East Antrim. Even if they do take a lot of silverware off us."

Jock raised his hat. "They're a good club," he observed. "Plenty o' loyal members." He took hold of his wife's arm. "Well, we must be getting on. See you next April."

He steered his wife down the embankment, her waxen fruitage waving in the wind.

V

One Saturday morning Colin was lounging luxuriously on Beth's settee, his inside warmed by a cup of coffee the gleaming appurtenances of which stood on the mantelpiece beside them. Beth, in a voluminous lavender sweater and tight black pants, flung herself on him like a cat and let her glossy hair down on his face, tickling him. The touch of his warm body was delightful to her.

"Horrible person," she said.

He raised his eyebrows in mock despair. "What have I done?"

"Nothing. That's the point, you've done nothing. At eleven-thirty in the morning you can think of nothing better to do than lounge revoltingly on this settee. You're an opossum."

"An opossum?"

"Yes. —They *are* lazy, aren't they?"

"No idea."

"Well I say they are. And what's more, you're one."

"How am I to wash this stain from my character?"

They decided to go to a rugby match. Heaven knew why, because Beth had a cultivated ignorance of the game. But Warnock remembered that Queen's had an important league match against Instonians at Ravenhill, and she agreed to go in a spirit of scientific enquiry. As for him, he looked forward to seeing Hunter, who had been doing great things in the Inter-Provincial series.

No sooner had they installed themselves in the big stand, surrounded by students with long blue scarves and nascent beards, than the bottom was ripped out of the sky. A deluge of

77

rain came down.

"We're devils for our pleasures," remarked Beth, wrinkling her nose and drawing her coat around her. It was cold, but the stand roof kept the rain off them.

Not so the players; their laundered jerseys were reduced to wet shapelessness in seconds. Hunter was captain of Queen's this season and led them out; in a moment the water was running down his ruddy face and standing in droplets in his hair; but he seemed to enjoy it.

The referee's whistle, starting the game, provoked a ragged cheer. Then the opposing packs flung themselves on each other and wrestled deliriously in the mud for forty minutes. The backs stood around with the hair plastered on their foreheads, and the spectators sat in glum silence. "Call this sport?" said Beth.

At the interval a figure in a threadbare black overcoat came scuttling up to them and sat down beside Warnock. "Colin," it said. "You're a stranger."

"Brendan!" Warnock felt a surge of pleasure, punctured by a pinprick of guilt; Foley was running for the cross-country team, had indeed taken his place at number one.

"What a day," he was saying, shaking his dark head. But there was a hint of pleasure on his face; rumour had it that he liked a good penance. The Irish weather certainly gave him plenty of opportunities.

"Do you know Beth McCann? Beth, this is Brendan Foley."

They said how-do-you-do, examining each other curiously. To ease the situation Warnock made a lame joke: "But, Brendan, won't you be thrown out of the Gaelic A. A. for watching rugby? You should be wearing a false moustache."

Foley smiled. "Watching's only a venial sin. If I caught the ball and threw it back that might be different."

"Jesuit!"

"To tell you the truth, I'm here to see Rex. They say he's quite a star."

Colin realised with a pang: affection has brought him here. He felt excluded, discriminated against.

The teams were lining up again. "I must be away now," said Foley. "I've got a friend down there." He made his way across a couple of lettered blocks to where a girl was sitting.

"Well, I'll be blowed," said Beth. "These religious types would surprise you." She slipped her hand secretly in Colin's pocket and squeezed his.

The teams had finished sucking their quarters of lemon and flung them in the general direction of the touch line; all fell short. Then the wrestling began again.

But, almost without anyone noticing, the rain had eased. As if in celebration the Queen's forwards bullocked up the field, engaged in an untidy catch-as-catch-can on the Instonians line and scored a scrambled try. This was greeted by a few sarcastic whoops; genuine applause came only when Hunter converted, sending the greasy ball cleanly between the uprights almost from the touch-line. It was a happy noise, with a conspiratorial tinge to it that made Warnock jealous. Bloody team sports, he thought.

A falsetto voice which had been calling forlornly for Queen's to run with the ball found the crowd agreeing with it. The players, willing to try anything once, strung together a few shaky movements; at last Hunter, playing at centre-three-quarter, received the ball cleanly, accelerated outside his man and made for the corner flag. The full-back made a despairing lunge at him but could not stop him. He ran in and grounded the ball under the posts.

Pandemonium among the students; their idol had scored. Beth's elbow dug into Warnock's side. "Hey, you men," she whispered urgently, "don't gang up on me!" If only she knew!

thought Colin; he felt as much out of it as she did. But he said nothing, merely giving her hand a squeeze.

The match over and Queen's the winners by ten points, they walked down the narrow gangway to ground level and shuffled towards the exit. One or two players had been delayed at the corner of the pitch, to give autographs. Rex was among them. As they approached he shooed the last schoolboy away and walked across the banked concrete steps to them. They exchanged a few words among the eddies of damp mackintoshes.

"You obliged as usual," said Colin.

"Ach, I was lucky. I got a good pass. But where have you been hiding? I haven't seen hilt nor hair of you for weeks."

Warnock was put out. "Oh, you know . . ."

"I know damned well!" Hunter looked at Beth and laughed hugely. Colin made shamefaced introductions and said: "I saw Brendan at half-time. I never knew he was the rugby type."

"He's not. We made a deal. He's here today and tomorrow I'm to break the Sabbath and watch Antrim playing Cavan at Gaelic. Think of it: a lot of hallions running along bouncing a football on their toe—and they have the nerve to call their ground Casement Park!"

He laughed again and rubbed his cheek, spreading an already broad smear of mud from the wing of his nose to the lobe of his ear. He was steaming in the cold air like a dray horse. "Here, Colin," he went on, more seriously, "what's up with you, not running in the cross-country?"

"I didn't feel like it."

"Fair enough. A lot of people say it's bad of you but I tell them to mind their own business."

"I've given up training for a couple of months." Then, in a burst of embittered confidence: "To tell you the truth, Rex, I don't even know whether I'll start up again in the spring. Why sweat your guts out for nothing?"

"Why indeed?" He looked at Beth meaningfully. "I wouldn't run a bloody inch myself if I didn't enjoy it. If you don't get any fun out of a thing, don't do it; that's my outlook." He clapped Warnock on the shoulder with a muddy palm. "Well, I must get changed." He walked off through the thinning crowd, his studs gnashing at the concrete.

Beth felt she liked him intensely.

VI

Her relationship with Warnock deepened and consolidated. It was a marriage, but a secret one. The secrecy, necessary on the material level, infected others. For example, Warnock drew back from visiting Limavady at Christmas. Beth did not insist on inviting him; in her heart she knew he wasn't ready. She took the train alone.

But she was back in the flat on New Year's Day. "Working in the library," she had told her father.

They resumed their love-making with a new knowingness; the days apart had crystallised their attitudes. For Beth, love was a flame on which she flung herself in exquisite agony to be consumed. In return, it gave her life a meaning: she *was* this particular act with this particular person. It reduced her to her woman's function, but that was enough. More than enough.

Colin was more male, more self-absorbed. For him love was an accession of power: a free gift of that ultimate strength he had failed to find on the track. In the crisis of physical pleasure his lust to assert himself was satisfied. When they lay together in the post-coital twilight, drained of personality, he felt serene and tolerant: love was a success story and he had the easy generosity of the successful. But Beth was wrung to tears. She would snuggle up to him, making herself small, and whisper haplessly: "I love you. Oh I love you."

One evening when he was getting ready to leave the flat she said drowsily: "You never talk about your mother. I'm beginning to think she doesn't exist."

"To tell you the truth, I don't think much about her. We've been apart for so long. I go over to Hamburg every summer to see her of course, but we're not close. She never was the sort of person to be interested in a child—even her own child."

"Tell just the same."

Colin hesitated for a moment. "I've got photographs of her. In Balmoral Avenue. Why don't we go there and look at them?"

Beth, supine on the settee, raised her head. "So I'm to beard the ghost of daddy in his den? All right then. Why not?"

He left her and drove down towards the Lisburn Road. Turning the corner into it, he saw a familiar figure hooked by the armpits to the railing of a house. It was tall and gaunt and even in stupor there was something unyielding about it.

He called out of the window. "Sam! Are you all right?"

No answer. He got out of the car and walked over. A man hurrying home glanced at them, decided what whatever was going on wasn't respectable and continued on his way.

"Sam!" He bent over the motionless figure and peered into its face. "Sam. For heaven's sake, say something."

A sepulchral voice replied: "Bugger you. Satisfied?"

Harbinson detached himself from the railing and dusted himself off unsteadily. He reeked of stout. Drawing himself up, he glared at Warnock through bloodshot eyes. "Why can't you leave a fellow alone? I was only having a wee rest."

"I'll take you home. Where do you live?"

"In Ballymena, you bloody fool."

"I meant, where are your digs?"

After a pause: "In Stockman's Lane. Just before the rugby ground."

"Get in."

Harbinson obeyed; he was being insulting only on the theoretical plane. He sank with a grunt into the bucket seat.

"It's hardly out of my way," said Warnock, driving across the Lisburn Road.

"Oh no?" said Harbinson, heavily ironic. He made a circular movement with his hand, signifying the car. "This is quicker than Shank's mare," he observed.

"Yes."

"And Windsor Avenue's a sight cosier than Cherryvale."

"I suppose so." Warnock was being preternaturally patient.

"What does old Solomon Schuhmacher say to all that?"

"I don't know. I haven't asked him."

Harbinson yawned into his hand. In a moment they were outside his house. He hauled himself out of the car. "I suppose I'd better say thanks," he said grudgingly.

Colin shrugged his shoulders and prepared to let out the clutch. Then he saw the other stagger to a lamppost and spew down the fluted green stem. He switched the engine off and got out.

Sam waved him away, produced a handkerchief from his pocket and wiped his mouth; Colin was assailed with the smell of vomit.

"Warnock, you're a bit of a bloody eejit but you're not a bad fellow."

He walked in at the gate of the house, shaken but sobering fast.

VII

Beth stepped through the front door of the house in Balmoral Avenue as gingerly as a cat on wet ground, mentally lifting her paws in distaste and giving them a little shake to remove the hostile element.

Mrs McArdle was waiting silently in the hall, imposing in her black velveteen dress; her grey-streaked hair was brushed tightly over her ears and twisted into a bun. She greeted Beth with all the decorum of a woman whose family had been in domestic service for generations. She represented a tradition; indeed she knew that it would die out with her. She was its last flowering.

"Very glad to meet you, Miss McCann. I'll take your coat." She hung the garment on the stand and opened the drawing room door. "Just step this way if you please. I've lit a fire for you. If it's not enough just ring and I'll bring the paraffin heater."

Beth murmured her thanks. She was used to a certain amount of ceremonial, but not this much. She sank into an armchair big enough to accommodate a giant, and giggled: "Oh Colin, it's like something out of Dickens. Or the deanery at Barchester."

"I must be used to it. It just seems the natural way for a house to be."

"And those spears! I thought—a governor general at least."

There was a discreet tap at the door. Colin said "Yes?" and Mrs McArdle returned with a tea trolley loaded with hot buttered scones, currant bread and Dundee cake. Its crowning glory was a strawberry flan: sponge cake, fresh strawberries and quivering jelly topped with whipped cream.

"How wonderful! Did you make it yourself?"

"Yes miss, thank you miss. —May I pour for you?" She filled two fine-bone china cups from what was obviously a Georgian silver teapot. "Mr Warnock's father—that is, Mr Colin's grandfather—had these." She backed her way out of the room.

Beth and Colin attacked the food; there was enough for half a dozen but they made hefty inroads into it, disposing of the flan in its entirety and downing three cups of tea.

"How do you feel—better?" Colin asked.

"Bloated. But ready to face the photos. Bring me to them."

"No. This house was built before the days of central heating, remember. I'll bring them to you." He went out.

Waiting for him in the blazing aura of the fire, drugged by the flickering patterns of light, Beth felt herself being hypnotised into a gentle torpor. The heat washed over her, relaxing her. Superficially she felt receptive to outside influences, but deep down she was falling asleep.

Colin came back with a shoebox tied with string. He undid the loops and took the lid off. Then Beth and he sat down together on the leopard-skin rug in front of the grate, and one by one he drew out his treasures.

"I found the box like this when we were going through his things. He'd put all these photos and mementoes together. It was touching: he must have cared for her even after she left him."

They saw a very young woman, blonde if you could trust the cockled, yellowing photograph, with full, sensuous lips. She was wearing a heavily belted coat. "She's beautiful," said Beth. "But why are the cheeks so thin?"

"She was starving, I suppose. This was Germany in 1945. She was twenty and training to be a singer in Leipzig when the Russians came. She had to leave everything. Funny to think how her property—or what's left of it—and Klaus Schuhmacher's are circulating somewhere in East Germany at this moment!"

"Did they know each other?"

"Not personally. He left in '33, you see. But the families knew each other. Her maiden name was Klose: Irmgard Klose, though she calls herself Laura Manzini on the stage. The Kloses, I'm glad to say, had a good war. No party members, and helped their Jewish friends discreetly. Nothing heroic, of course, but decent."

"She went to Hamburg then?"

"Yes. She had some idea of moving on to Sweden if things didn't work out, but she never did. Father took care of that."

Beth, languidly content, looked at the photograph: was there any resemblance? No; he was a scaled down, domesticated version of his father; *her* contribution was more the refining and sensitising of the Warnock face. But that spoiled look she sometimes surprised in his eyes, that persistent intellectual discontent, was surely a continental thing.

"It was the time of the cigarette economy," Colin said. "The opera house had been bombed and was nowhere near re-opening. They were talking about using the old stage as an auditorium and rigging up a makeshift one, but it hadn't happened yet. The standard occupation for good-looking girls was sleeping with British officers."

Beth pointed to the photograph. "That explains the coat. It's military, isn't it?"

"Don't jump to conclusions! Father gave it to her. She was lucky; she met him three days after she arrived."

"I like this," said Beth drowsily. "I mean, your father sharing his cloak with his beloved. I was frightened of him. Now I'm not any more." She snuggled up to Colin on the rug and said: "More please."

He told her how his father had come to be in Hamburg, days after the city was taken: he was in charge of food supplies in the British Zone of Occupation and *de facto* minister of agriculture for a third of Germany. "It was enough to kill most men, for him just another job."

"What do you mean, *another*? Wasn't he a kind of monolith?"

"Far from it. He was very impulsive, couldn't settle at anything. He would take one job, squeeze it dry and then move on to another."

The trip to Kenya had been his break-through; his book had been a minor sensation in academic circles. He was called back to Belfast to fill the newly created Chair of Agriculture at Queen's, and after a few years there went off to London to be Head of the Northcott Research Institute, where he formulated the other great, simple principle with which his name was associated: to eradicate malnutrition was not enough, responsible governments must aim at giving the poor as varied and nourishing a diet as the well-to-do; the absence of *ill* health did not imply *good* health. "When I came out with that they hailed me as an original thinker," he would snort. "After four thousand years of human civilisation!"

His unsolicited advice to governments was a straw in the wind. He turned to politics in his spare time and was elected as an independent M.P. to the university seat at Queen's, performing as a rogue-elephant liberal with a socialist tinge. He served on endless committees: committees for the reorganisation of the milk industry, the fat-stock industry, the fishing industry. After five years of back-breaking work he suddenly kicked himself free and retired to his farm at Crawfordsburn to write another, bigger book. He called it *A Law Of Peace*, after a pronouncement of Pasteur, whom he admired:

> Two opposing forces seem to be in conflict: the one a law of blood and death, offering each day new

87

modes of destruction, forces nations to be always ready for battle; the other a law of peace, work and health whose only aim is to deliver man from the calamities which beset him. Which of these laws will prevail God knows.

In the book he finally fused the practical and theoretical bents of his mind, calling in round terms on the nations of the earth to institute a world food plan or face the end of civilisation.

The book appeared on September 3rd 1939 and was forgotten in the patriotic stampede. Not that Robert cared: he was too busy besieging the offices of the mighty in search of work. He was put in charge of the food supply of all the south-eastern counties of England, and later became chairman of a Committee On Food Policy which could truthfully claim at war's end that the country's diet had been better under rationing than it had even been in peacetime.

Robert had not waited to claim these laurels. Restless as ever, he had resigned in 1944 to become Food Advisory Officer to the British armies, then in France. Somehow he still found time to write; a number of pamphlets kept his name before the public. Then, in the spring of 1945, when people were beginning to think about the kind of world they wanted when the war was over, *A Law Of Peace* was reissued and caught the prevailing mood. He became famous.

And so he came to Hamburg, a celebrated man and a "character"—the sort who can't keep out of the newspapers.

"He was in his prime really," Colin said reflectively, "and completely heart-whole."

"What? You don't mean he'd never had anything to do with women?" Beth sat up incredulously.

The question came to Warnock from another world; he was deep in his father's universe. He laughed sheepishly. "No, I don't mean that. He'd had a lot of affairs, but never married. It was all just an overflow from his other activities. He'd never been in love."

But he was, painfully, with Irmgard. The conquering invader, famous, still vigorous, with craggy good looks, succumbed to the impoverished young singer. "She fancied herself in love with him. Maybe she even was. At any rate she became his mistress the day after they met and in a month they were married. The papers were full of it."

"Why not? It's a great story."

"It couldn't last though. They were both too egotistical, too wilful. Mother too—she's as tough as old boots under the artistic gush. And he was completely indifferent to music, not to mention musicians. How he ever made a friend of Schuhmacher is a mystery. Perhaps he needed the contrast."

"I must meet your mother," declared Beth, striking a dramatic attitude on the rug.

"You will, but . . . oh, honestly, I don't know that you'll like her very much. Opera singers have capacious gullets. They swallow everything around them. She'll swallow *you* and when she tires of it she'll spit you out."

"Charming image."

"True, unfortunately. When I go to see her I'm always delighted for a day or two. Then I get out of sorts. It's such a battle—she races you round to see her friends, books you into all her performances, whisks you off to the seaside. Talking sixteen to the dozen all the time and never listening to what you have to say in return. How an impatient man like father stood her for six years is one of the miracles of our time. Especially after she had to give up her career."

"Of course—when he became V.C. here. In a city without an opera!"

"Exactly. She thought we were a bunch of barbarians and

said so to everybody in sight, from visiting cabinet ministers to the Lord Mayor. She hectored men forty years older than she was. Father would bellow and say that if she was still keen on music he'd buy her a penny whistle. She once threw her finger bowl at him, at some dinner or other. Finally she just left and started singing again."

Beth laughed. "Well, I think she's splendid. And if ever they make you V.C. I'll do the same to you. —Now let's look at some more of those snaps."

They looked at Robert, grim and forbidding—he always refused to smile-please—and Irmgard, well-fed now and looking spoiled. Her earlier, thinner self wore the exaggeratedly long dresses of the New Look; as she got plumper the hem line rose. Here she was, full-bosomed in a bathing costume on some Mediterranean beach, here with her arms flung alluringly round the neck of her grumpy husband, here in a cart-wheel hat at a garden party.

And here she was with a baby in her arms! Anonymous enough, thought Beth, peering closely, but her diaphragm turned to water to see her standing up this little boy of three— oh, unmistakably Colin, with those serious dark eyes—on a chair to be snapped.

She glanced involuntarily towards him now. He was bent over the shoe box, arranging its contents. He looked up at her: the eyes were exactly the same: serious, a little dreamy, with long lashes. Wrung with love and pity, she kissed him. Even the menace of Mrs McArdle could not quell them; they made love on the spot, their skins pink from the glow of the fire.

Beth went to bed that night glad that she had braved the Warnock house; the ghosts it contained were not so fearsome after all—just pictures on little pieces of paper. She might even make something quite presentable of the place when it was hers. She slept sound.

No so Colin. When he came back from leaving her home the fire which had made a charmed circle for them had died down; the ghosts walked again. Selfish, obsessed ghosts both of them; one that neglected him and one that pulverised him. He had come to terms with the first years ago; but he brooded on the other, the one with the long shadow, deep into the night.

VIII

His housekeeper put a letter on his breakfast plate the following morning. The angular hand was Schuhmacher's. He tore it open and read:

> Colin,
>   Please come and see me tomorrow morning. I need your signature on some legal documents concerning the transfer of your father's estate. I shall be in my room from ten o'clock.
>   K. S.

The room was directly below the German lecture room in University Square. It was upholstered with books from floor to ceiling; the only gaps were for the door and window. The desk was so placed that Schuhmacher could look out through his lace curtains at the postage-stamp garden with its stunted tree of exotic appearance (it looked like a magnolia under a curse) and the university complex beyond.

When Colin appeared he was standing behind this desk with his glasses balanced on his nose. Half a dozen open books and some type-written slips of paper were laid out neatly on the mahogany surface in front of him.

"Colin," he said, "do come in. I was just writing a lecture; hence these quotations. As you know, I'm a great man for the synoptical view. —Now, where have I put those documents? Ah yes . . ."

He opened a drawer and took out three heavy wads of grey-blue paper written over in copperplate. "You must sign all three and in addition initial each paragraph. I shall witness your signature. These things would normally be done in Mr Causley's presence, but as he's been the family solicitor for so long . . . I told him you might not want to go to his office just now." He blinked and adjusted his glasses.

The window had a broad wooden shelf in front of it, a relic of the house's former state before partitions were thrown up and doorways gouged in masonry walls. Colin took the documents over to this improvised table and scribbled his signature and initials where Schuhmacher had indicated; while he did so the professor returned to his slips of paper and jotted down a note or two in his ledger-like book. When Colin had finished he took the documents and added his signature as witness.

As he was putting everything back in his drawer the telephone rang. "Excuse me. —Hello?"

Colin's eyes wandered over this academic den, taking in the essay scripts in a pile on the floor, the occasional table stacked with formidable looking periodicals in Gothic type. He could smell the dusty odour, mingled with a faint aroma of glue and paper, that hangs around books.

". . . I agree with you, Harold, but you know the attitude the bursar is likely to take. I cannot see the slightest hope of our library grant being raised at the expense of other departments. Still, we can try . . ."

Inter-departmental politics. Ugh. Colin took a book from the shelves, a study of Michelangelo's sculpture with sumptuous photographs, and leafed over it till the phone call showed signs of coming to an end.

". . . agreed. But why don't you ring Margaret? She's very much the English specialist but may be sympathetic . . . Very well. Are you lunching in the common room? . . . Good, I'll see you there."

He put down the receiver. "Now, Colin, sit down while I talk to you." Colin returned Michelangelo to his shelf. "I want to advise you, as a friend. Will you let me do that?"

Warnock nodded; the request was too modest to decline. But there was a sinking feeling in the pit of his stomach, as when he had been caught doing something naughty as a child, and he resented that: why should he be ashamed? He was twenty-one after all; he had the vote.

Schuhmacher said, in his gentlest voice: "Do you realise you are being unfair to this girl? —No, don't be angry; I didn't say you were doing it on purpose."

Colin's eyes fell on one of the quotation slips: *Is it not better to fall into the hands of a murderer than into the dreams of a lustful woman?*

"I have, to my regret, no knowledge of woman in that special sense." Schuhmacher smiled his secret smile. "But I do know that one should not enter into a contract without the honest intention of fulfilling it. You believe you do so intend, but you are mistaken."

Warnock breathed deeply, struggling to control himself. And succeeded, if only for the moment.

"You see, Colin, I know you well enough to realise that your primary loyalty is not to other people, even those you love. It is to yourself and your ideals. At this stage in your life those ideals centre in your running. Very powerfully too. You imagine you have given them up but it is not so. You have merely suspended them in your disappointment and—I'm sorry for the word—pique."

. . . One day you will no longer see your noble part; your baseness you will see all too clearly. . .

"At your age any temporary defeat means humiliation. I know that. But when you are as old as I am you will no longer be sure which events in your life were defeats and which were victories. The taste of humiliation will have become familiar; it will cause you no more than the faintest malaise. You will not worry about defeats. You *will* worry about turning away from what you know you must do. Because that is cowardice."

"Cowardice!"

"Let me finish. I am not suggesting that you give up the enjoyment of real life for some will-o'-the-wisp. But every man has his priorities, and you have yours. So why allow this girl to blind herself as to what they are—is that honest? Is it fair? You belong to a special race: one that is compelled to measure itself against a self-imposed ideal and will sacrifice anyone or anything to that process."

Schuhmacher folded his hands in his lap, and fell silent. His face was concerned, almost apologetic; yet there was something indomitable about it: an indomitable mildness.

Colin's flash of anger had subsided. Klaus Schuhmacher was a second father to him; how could he be angry with him? But he was still hurt. "Why are you trying to make one of your intellectual heroes out of me? You've no right."

"True. But if I had been totally off the point you would not have felt it necessary to make this protest."

Warnock made an impatient gesture towards the slips of paper on the desk. "I'm no Nietzsche. Please don't cast me as one." His indignation rose again as he spoke. "Why must you always try to make me fit into *your* concept of life? I refuse to be a puppet, even one of your heroic ones. Leave your heroics to people who believe in them."

Schuhmacher's eyes dropped; Colin realised he had hurt

him. After a moment he spoke again. "This is a grave accusation, Colin." He took a handkerchief from his pocket, removed his spectacles and slowly polished the lenses. "We all try to influence other people, of course. But you imply that I have gone beyond the normal limits. You accuse me of moral blackmail."

"I don't think I went that far . . . Well, all right, I did. I'm sorry." Why did he feel it necessary to apologise? He was the injured party after all.

"It is I that am sorry. But will you admit that I have not used anything that was not already in yourself?"

"All blackmailers do that."

"True. But the motives are different. As far as I know, blackmailers don't act in the victim's best interests." He sketched his little smile.

"Meaning that you do?"

"Yes."

"All right then. Granted all this—which, by the way, I *don't* grant—that I'm letting the side down, funking what I'm failing at: what does it matter anyway? In a hundred years who's going to care?"

"Nobody. Not a living soul."

Colin was shocked out of his annoyance. He looked up.

"You were expecting some pious platitude, I suppose. Nothing is lost in the sight of God—something of that nature: an up-to-date version of the heavenly reward. Unfortunately I don't believe in the heavenly reward. Any success you have will last just as long as the headlines of the Sunday newspaper. As for your hundred years—in that time you and your achievements will be as irrevocably dead as myself."

Colin blushed; it had never occurred to him that Schuhmacher might be devoid of illusions.

"No. The pursuit of the ideal doesn't lead to anything. There is a sort of *practical* idealism that does; but that was your father's province, not yours. I want to see you running again, but not under false pretences. As a purely gratuitous activity."

"Perhaps you're right. Maybe I *am* one of those tiresome people who keep on nagging away at a thing until they're satisfied they've got it right. But I'm not sure; I'm confused. I don't know what sort of person I am any more."

"I do."

"You're very sure of yourself."

"Of you."

Colin sighed. "Don't, Klaus. I need time. I need to be left alone."

"In that case there's no more to be said. For the present."

Schuhmacher gave him an embarrassed little pat on the shoulder; they smiled at each other. Good; they were parting as friends. But Colin felt exhausted; his only thought was Beth: see Beth, touch Beth. But Beth was away, spending the day with Patricia Orr and her parents. Just when he needed her most.

For the first time, he felt some sympathy for the magnolia tree in the wretched garden.

IX

It froze hard during the night and the following morning dawned cold and clear. Early February brings days like that in Ireland: days when the sky is a pure aqueous blue, chilly and remote,and the sun shines with brightness but no warmth on a frost-bound land.

It is weather that calls for scarves and walking shoes. Before breakfast Colin had telephoned Beth and arranged to go out in the afternoon. They drove up into the Castlereagh hills and left the car at a crossroads where a signpost pointed four dilapidated fingers slightly askew.

Now that she was out Beth felt less than enthusiastic. She had been sweltering all morning in the heat of a coal fire. Lizard-like, she needed the heat; the emotional high of the last few weeks had left her feeling cold and drained. And out here it was even colder! She shivered, and pulled her coat collar up.

"Come on," said Colin briskly. "You need warming up." He led her off, his boots coming down on the asphalt of the little road with a series of small reports that carried in the still air but sent back no echo. He felt great physical well-being; he could walk all day like this and never tire.

They were in the drumlin country of North Down, an endless succession of small rounded hills where the glaciers had ground the landscape into clay hummocks before a warmer age drove them back; the little domes were covered in a green velvet of grass and dotted with gaunt clusters of trees. It is a quaint, rather stylised landscape; the sort of thing you would expect a toy train to run through in an eccentric's attic. To the left there were occasional glimpses of Belfast Lough, the water sparkling like a brilliant, with here and there a ship leaving its scribble of smoke on the clear sky.

Ordinarily a day like this would have invigorated Beth. The cold air, like a retort full of icy crystals, would have run through her veins and made her want to do crazy things: smash somebody's window or run naked across a respectable lawn. But today it wasn't like that. "I'm just not in the mood," she thought crossly.

To make matters worse, Colin was striking out powerfully, giving his body the pleasure of action. "Let's turn off here!" he called from twenty yards ahead of her and plunged into a lane that burrowed its way along the hollow between two hills. Why he chose that particular one he hardly knew. It seemed the natural thing to do. The place had something remotely familiar about it.

They were in the shade now, and the earth was flinty under-foot. In the open fields they could see how the frost had at last melted into a million drops of light that hung on the thistles and naked hawthorn twigs. But here in the lane a white rime still dusted the grass-blades and the brown scars of earth. They put down their feet by sudden deep cart ruts, or startling holes where a cow's hoof had torn through the soil: these relics of summer had dirty shells of ice, perilously thin, where yesterday's water had frozen and seeped away. A dried crust of dung had been lifted an inch from the earth by the slow-growing grass.

They said nothing. Beth had nothing to say and Colin was oddly puzzled; he felt he was walking in a dream. The sense of familiarity was growing: had the lane knowingly drawn them into it? And if so, towards what? He was walking automatical-ly now, without conscious volition.

Coming round a bend, he realised. "Beth!" he called, with subdued excitement. "Do you know where we are? I'm a fool not to have recognised it, but I've never come at it from this side before. We're at the farm."

"The *what*?" His tone of voice irritated her; there was awe in it, as though they were approaching a shrine.

"The farm. You know, our old family place. I used to spend half the summer here when I was a boy. It's let out now, to an ex-naval officer. A very good tenant."

"That's a comfort," said Beth drily.

They climbed over a gate into a field that sloped steeply up to a bald crown topped with a hedge. "There's not an acre of flat land hereabouts," said Colin, portentous as a tourist guide. "Drumlins all the way, packed as tight as eggs in a box."

The fields were all small affairs, no more than an acre or two, all tilted, all rising to the summit of their particular hill.

"What do they *grow* here anyway?" Beth asked in an irritated voice. This was Robert Warnock country. His ghost haunted it. Her woman's weapons were no use here.

"Nothing; it's all pastoral. There's a herd of fifty cows: all indoors now, on straw. They average over five hundred gallons of milk a year. Or did when I was a child; no doubt there have been improvements since. —Oh and look, there *is* one ploughed field. Just as I thought, eastern-facing. For new potatoes."

"Oh."

"Yes. The morning sun melts the frost and protects them." He went on, pedagogic again: "You don't usually have market gardening here. That's down to the south-east, around Newtownards."

"I didn't know you were such a specialist."

"I had to be. Otherwise I'd never have had an iota of respect from Father. Not that I *did* have much. —Look, there's the corner of the barn. The outhouses are just the same; the new man hasn't changed anything."

They walked on till they could see the house itself, an attractive mongrel pile, something between a farm house and country manse, with a rose garden to one side. "You can see the wing grandfather put on when we were beginning to get respectable," said Colin excitedly. "Oh Beth, let's ring the bell, shall we?"

"No." Something in her rebelled against this pervasive aura of family—a family that shut guests out instead of welcoming them in, as her own did. But then her own was composed of ordinary human beings, personalities of average potency; this one was made up of Robert Warnock, a genius and her enemy. "No, I don't want to."

"But it would be lovely. We'd be sure to be invited in for tea. We could see my old room."

"I don't want to see your old room and I don't want tea," she suddenly burst out. "This place is hateful, hateful!"

Colin was astounded. "But Beth . . . Honestly . . . I just

99

don't see . . ."

She stamped her foot, literally. "You'd see if you weren't so wrapped up in that damned family of yours. For all the attention you pay me I might as well be on the moon. You just don't know I'm here!"

"That's not fair. I was trying to show you something interesting. I thought you would . . . "

"Well you thought wrong. I don't care tuppence about all the Warnocks in the world. I don't want to hear any more about your father. Or your uncles. Or your cousins. Or anybody. I wish to God you'd never had a father!" She burst into tears: tears of rage, tears at annoyance at herself for feeling it.

Colin turned pale, then his cheeks reddened. "What have you got against my father?"

Between the sobs she blurted out: "You think a sight more about him dead than me alive. You're obsessed with him, obsessed with a dead man."

"Is that all you can find to pick a quarrel over?" he said, his voice full of suppressed anger.

"I can find a lot." She blew her nose into a little white handkerchief edged with lace; the river of black hair shook with each movement of her head. "When you make love to a girl you ought to have honest intentions."

"But I wanted us to be engaged!"

"Engaged? You're engaged to your precious father. And to that pretentious old phoney Schuhmacher. You might have explained that I was only going to get their left-overs."

Colin shouted in sudden fury: "Damn you! Damn all women! They're not content with your body, they must have your soul as well." He smacked one fist into the palm of the other hand.

"Keep your miserable little soul. Keep your body too. Who ever asked you for it? Keep it to your rotten little self."

But she *had* asked him for it, and he was outraged. "Don't pretend you're so indifferent to my body," he cried scornfully, seizing her by the wrists. "Would you like a list of times and dates?"

Beth flinched as though he had hit her. He himself, overcome with the enormity of what he had said, stared stupidly at a stone in front of him on the ground. When he had plucked up the courage to look up he realised that she hadn't moved, but was standing in the same position, head raised, arms held out slightly, arrested in mid-action. Tears were slowly welling out of her eyes. Shaking the stupefaction from him, he took a step towards her. But she turned her head away, denying him.

What had possessed him to say such a thing? As he pondered, the truth came to him: her reproach had stung him because it was the same one that Schuhmacher had made to him.

And each was right. He had betrayed them both: Schuhmacher by turning away from the ideal, Beth by using her as a comforter when the going got tough. He had never shared the most important part of his mind with her, the part where the real decisions were made. He wondered: am I incapable of ordinary domestic happiness? He didn't know the answer, but was sure of one thing: at this moment at least, love came lower in his order of priorities than whatever it was that made him run. He'd been living in a fool's paradise, denying his own nature and in the end hurting this girl whom he loved.

Well, he would deny himself no longer; he would do what had to be done. He looked questioningly at Beth, they turned back without a word and walked slowly through the cold tunnel of the lane to the road and the car. They were exhausted from the spill of emotion.

The drive was short and silent. They parted at her door with a single muffled goodnight.

Chapter 3

I

"So it's you?"

Jock barked the words out over the sudden bitten-off shouts, the slap of rubber soles on the gym floor: irregular patterings, like rain-drops, running together in a sudden flurry as the defence closed in on an attacker trying to wriggle clear. The ball twanged against the iron rim of the basket. Every sound reverberated from the glass roof; the climbing-ropes, snaking down against the wall bars where they had been pushed out of the way, vibrated in time.

"Yes," said Colin. Unnecessarily, but he had to say something: he was standing there in his tweed sports coat and flannels with his shoes in his hand: great inflexible brogues that glowered reproach in this the domain of the slender basketball boot.

Jock turned away from the players, his referee's whistle

swinging on its white tape. "You know damn fine I cannae do anything now. Athletics at two as usual."

"I know, but I wanted to see if it was all right . . ."

"If what was all right?"

"Coming back. You don't mind, do you?"

"Don't talk balls. I'm paid for it, amn't I?" He saw something out of the corner of his eye, whipped the whistle to his lips and blew a blast. "Foul there, Wilson! Go for the ball, not the man. Free throw."

The game restarted; a lanky youth in long British-style shorts dropped the ball in a slow arc on to the basket-rim, where it ricocheted from side to side and popped out: no score.

"What brought you this far anyway?" asked Jock. The gym was a good half mile from the university, in a short avenue called—with unconscious irony—Sans Souci Park.

"I just came. I didn't have a lecture . . ."

"Since when has that bothered you? I heard you'd bid the academic life a last farewell."

"I started again this week."

Jock scratched the pad of ginger hair at the collar-opening of his jersey and grinned. "Off again, on again, eh? You all over, Colin."

Warnock, embarrassed, said nothing. The ball thumped against the backboard and dropped neatly into the basket: a point. "Don't let it go to your head, Purdy!" called Jock to the scorer as the teams lined up for the restart. "Like I said, two o'clock. Same arrangements as before—you work with Hunter and Foley. If you're able, that is." He looked up sharply. "But see here, laddie. We'd better have a wee agreement. Just between ourselves, mind, but something you'll keep. I've no love of bringin' an athlete up to peak condition just tae see him throw in his hand for damn all. I was bloody mad, and that's a fact. So next time you feel like skipping off we'll talk it over, if you please."

Being prepared for this didn't make it any easier to bear. Colin mumbled: "All right. Anything you want."

"Ach, son, I don't want to rub it in. But I need to know I'm no wastin' my time. So promise you'll stick it out unless I say go."

"I promise."

"Just remember that when it starts to hurt." Then, reaching over, he clapped Colin on the shoulder and said: "OK, laddie. Off with you. Cherryvale at two, like I said."

The subject was closed. Turning towards the door, Colin heard a whistle-blast and a pregnant obscenity. "Holy God, Jackson, the minute I turn my back you unlearn the very elements of the game . . ." He closed the door on laughter and chaff, sat down on a bench and put on his shoes.

II

It was a bitter February day. Colin stepped out of the pavilion into a Cherryvale that was half awash in fog: a thin, still fog trembling on the brink of freezing, hanging around the roots of the high hedges, stumping the outlines of the black skeleton trees. A heavy sky weighed on the rows of middle-class villas, withdrawn now into anonymity: only the parallel lines of smoke creeping painfully upwards showed that their dripping shells harboured life. It was almost dark already and their interiors full of shadows, but no lights were switched on: what decent housewife would waste current at two in the afternoon?

As the four figures trotted across to the track their nostrils steamed conical clouds at an angle of thirty degrees to the horizontal. The grass under their feet had had its living urge cut back by the season and was shrunk to a yellow caricature of itself, huddled up as it were for survival; green self-expression was not to be thought of. Colin noticed how sparse it had become in its winter state; gleaming black mud was apparent through it like a scalp through thinning hair.

"Just the stuff to make you pick your feet up." said Jock. "When you get on to cinders you'll think it's a picnic."

Rex was at home on such a surface; he sold an imaginary dummy, sprinted ten yards and, turning his hip into some opponent, threw a twenty-five yard pass to the gingerly trotting Warnock. Foley shuffled demurely forward, spending no unnecessary energy.

They flung off their track suits and ran on the spot, kicking their knees high and sawing with their arms to keep warm.

Jock examined Warnock's physique critically. "You're flabby, laddie. You'll never make a Billy Bunter but there's a good seven pounds to come off. I want to see you hungry-looking." He added, more gently: "Still it could be worse. You've been doing some walking at any rate."

"How about me?" shouted Rex, his limbs flailing. "Do I look hungry?"

"You look bleddy self-satisfied." Hunter, delighted, laughed. "Now come on—a couple o' laps easy striding. Colin lad, you're in for a tough afternoon. These two hallions are fit. Stay with them if you can. No half measures this late in the day. You've got exactly five months to reach your peak and for the next couple o' weeks you're damned well going to feel it."

As if to contradict him Warnock's spirits started to rise. His blood was flowing faster and the cold air on his warming, imperceptibly perspiring body was something he had come to think of as native to him; he had been denied it for three months now. He loped round the laps with the others, laughing and joking. Hunter gave him a shove and pretended to duck when Jock, Teddy-bear-like in his track suit, shook a jocular fist. Foley smiled his taut little smile and said: "Good to see you out again, Colin." Warnock was absurdly happy: a man reunited with long-lost loved ones.

But when they had finished their three laps he found his breath coming thick.

"Arm-sawing in pairs!" called Jock. Hunter faced Foley and laced his fingers through his; Warnock did the same with Jock himself. "Now!"

They looked each other in the eye and drove their arms, forward and back, forward and back, faster and faster. Colin felt Jock's crude male strength invade his body through the joined fingers. Unable to keep up the pace, he lost control.

"Don't be a jess! You'll never thrust home at the end of a race till you can move your fists like a flyweight. Again."

Again the harsh humiliation, again and again. At last—after only five minutes?—release. "Now for Colin's benefit, running on the spot again. One minute continuous." The first beading of sweat was breaking out on Warnock's body.

This kind of exercise was meat and drink to Rex. Leaning eagerly forward, he hammered his feet down in a long powerful burst, his whole frame quivering with urgency to move. Foley's rhythm was as discreet and unemphatic as his running: he kept his feet surprisingly low but maintained the pace relentlessly. As for Colin, he broke down: his sense of rhythm had gone to pot. A second start, fluffed. The third time he managed, but three starts in a minute was bad.

Heartbeat high, in the eighties at least. His face was slightly chop-fallen now, the first sign of fatigue, and his legs were sodden and unresponsive. The others were revelling in it, as well they might: the real training had not yet begun.

Jock looked at his watch and said: "Right, lads, now down to business. Sixteen two-twenties at thirty-one seconds apiece. Easy stuff." Colin groaned inwardly. "The interval's a generous one—the length of time it takes Colin to get back to his mark." Hunter grinned sarcastically, Foley with sympathy.

They all knew what was coming. Physiologically stated, they would be expanding their circulo-respiratory efficiency; in human terms it meant forcing yourself to run when you were already exhausted and then running again. You pushed your body to the limits of what it could bear in order to make it a tool.

Once, when Rex had complained at being meted out such treatment, Jock had told them a story: a famous runner, while still a schoolboy, ran twenty miles and finished in tears. When someone asked him what he was crying for he said: "It hurts so much." That he was free to stop had simply not occurred to him.

In effect he was not free, nor were they. Day after day, month after month, they would ignore the clamour of tissue for rest and force themselves to do what was impossible yesterday. There was no alternative; they had seen too many athletes—themselves included—crumple on the track, gutted of will-power, raped in the deepest part of them, their aspirations—ever to rebel against it. Each time they finished a schedule and stood there trembling and wan Jock would make light of it all with a quip. That would be their sole reward.

Thirty-one seconds for the first furlong was child's play. They ran it easily, then walked across the diameter of the track, back to the start. "Thirty point five," Jock called, his eye on his watch. "Too fast." Foley nodded earnestly. "I thought as much," he said. Colin was blowing, but not seriously.

A minute later they had started on another. This time it was a full two seconds too slow. "Thank Christ it's only February," complained Jock. "You're babes in arms as far as knowledge of pace is concerned. —Off you go again, don't dawdle!"

They ran a third and a fourth and a fifth. Colin was still able to stay with the others but had developed an excruciating stitch. Jock cocked an eye at him under his heavy brows as if daring him to drop out; he gritted his teeth and swore he would show nothing.

The interval between the furlongs worked out at about a minute and a half. They would finish, hear the time from Jock, cross the width of the track and start again. Once Colin found himself on the outside of a bend, covering yards more than the others. The stitch was unbearable; he felt he was running doubled up at the waist. Surely they would see the agony he was in? In fact they saw nothing. He finished, sprawling like a rag doll. Turning slowly, he found them already on the way back to the start. Head down, he followed.

"Thirty-one flat. Not bad. Eight more to go."

To Warnock each race seemed to last minutes longer than the one before. As they got up to nine, ten, eleven, the blood sang in his head and he thought he was going to faint. He managed to keep in contact with the others by dint of an effort that he thought would tear his body in two. He could hear nothing for the roaring in his ears, see nothing but the track at his feet. Each time they stopped he wandered blindly back to his position; should it kill him he would not keep them waiting, as Jock had taunted. He was running on a mixture of will-power and the memory of past races, the knowledge that the body is always capable of an extra ounce of effort. When it betrays, it betrays suddenly, in a faint. He knew he had to distrust the evidence of his senses, battered as they were and longing for peace.

They settled to their marks for the twelfth time. No words now; only the dry rasp of breathing. Foley's eyes wore a dull gloss: this was what he loved and feared, the triumph of the spirit over the body, the burning away of matter in a self-inflicted purgatory.

Colin's knees were strangely swollen. In the split second between Jock's hand signal and their wrenching themselves forward he realised he was on the brink of collapse. He staggered as they rose from their marks and cannoned into Rex, almost sending him flying. His arms were locked at the elbows; he put his whole mind to untying them, letting them move loosely at his sides. Staying upright seemed to depend on that.

No winners here. At the finish all three of them stood bent double, their hands on their knees. They went stiffly back to where Jock stood, Colin walking in a red haze.

"Fall out, Colin, you've had your whack. Do some deep breathing."

Warnock looked up aggrieved—but in the dizzy regions he now moved in did being aggrieved mean anything? He planted his aching feet thirty inches apart and inhaled.

Foley and Hunter ran another furlong, Hunter rousing himself from a state of prostration in which his head hung down as though on a string. This kind of repetition wore him out; he was built for splurging energy in a three-quarter-minute burst.

As they ran Jock said: "Not bad, Colin. I thought I'd have to stop you sooner." There was real respect in his voice.

"Nothing wrong with me." Pure bravado; the spots dancing before his eyes had yet to steady and disappear. While he was doing the blessed breathing exercise the others ran four other furlongs, completing two miles of running.

"All three of you—walk and jog! Keep moving!" Jock shooed them round the track, refusing them rest. You could see Hunter's spirits rise now the damned treadmill was over. Strength was flowing back to him; he was fetching up huge breaths from the pit of his stomach as through drawing them up from a well. Foley took the air in through his nose alone; it was a fetish of his, he believed his helped him get back to normal.

Twice they jogged round—or was it three times? Warnock's heart was still thudding uncomfortably when he heard Jock say: "Two four-forties, maximum output, interval as short as you can make it. You too, Colin; then you can call it a day while the others get on with their individual work period."

This time he really was aggrieved. "Isn't that a bit stiff for February?"

Jock thrust forward his underlip and said drily: "Things have been happening while you've been gallivanting—or hadn't you heard?"

"Heard what?"

"World records, that's what."

"So what?"

"Listen, son. The mile and the half both went in Australia six weeks ago."

"I know."

"Then you ought to bleddy well realise that it means trouble. You're going to have to run faster than you thought."

"All right, but what's the hurry?"

"Christ, laddie, you know as well as I do that when one man starts to run fast all the others follow suit—then his times get taken for granted. I'm telling you now: by December there'll be half a dozen milers capable of breaking 3:50. If you're to stand a chance with them you're going to have to get down to around 3:52 this summer. Only one way to do that: systematic training and hard work. I provide the one and you the other. So get to your mark."

They got down roughly, not using blocks. Colin was breathing more easily by now, but by the time they were off he knew he was capable of no more than a bear-like shamble over the wet grass. No amount of effort could win the battle of keeping in touch; Hunter, recovered now, was devouring the track with his rangy lope, crushing imaginary opposition at that fiendish distance where speed and strength as separate gifts are valueless: only a combination of both will do. Foley stayed with him, shuffling along flat-footed as he always did, heels and arms much too low for the purist. Seventy yards from home he made a spurt, got on momentary terms with Rex only to wilt under his merciless finish. Colin came home twenty yards behind, running on a mixture of pride, glue and red-hot cinders.

They were all three visibly drained of energy now. Hunter stared at the ground ten yards in front of him, Foley had the beginnings of a white line on his lips. "Forty-eight point five, Rex," Jock called. "It'll just about do. But don't hang around in the middle of the race. —Are you all ready?"

They ran it again. This time Rex could manage only forty-nine. Jock blinked like an ancient owl, his eyes dissatisfied under their hoods. "You're falling off. —Now walk and jog. I'm coming with ye."

Colin's world was empty of light. Cherryvale, its rugby pitches and tennis courts, were black before his eyes. The sky was black too, but a black of lesser intensity. Sight and sound seemed to come to his brain cells through a cataract, a roaring of water that resolved itself into a blinding headache. It was the best part of a minute before he could take in what Jock was saying.

"Good, Colin, good. You're in better shape than I feared. And I can see you're serious this time. —Here, have a glucose drink, it's settling." They walked round the grass circuit a couple of times. The noise in Warnock's head lessened, allowing his senses to get purchase on the natural world: he saw colours again as colours. Perspective, which had deserted him, glided back. Things came into focus.

Jock was saying: "You know, you're our problem child just now. The others are well advanced and they have their other training besides: Brendan's got his cross-country and Rex his rugby—he's playing against Scotland next week. But you're nowhere. I can't hold them back, you understand? You'll have to catch up as you may."

In front of them Hunter was cracking some joke to Foley, raising his hand in self-salutation, laughing. "Like I said, I'm giving you 3:52 to aim at. By mid-July or thereabouts—in time for the A.A.A. Championships or one of those big meetings at the White City."

Warnock was utterly exhausted; he felt as though he was walking through treacle. Each foot had to be dragged out of a sucking resistant mass. His abdominals were so tender that he couldn't jog; he trotted along stiff-kneed as though frightened his shorts might fall down.

But Jock wasn't giving him any respite. "At this moment," he went on, "you couldn't do *four* fifty-two, but nae matter. We'll soon set that to rights. In a week's time I want to see you starting on a schedule I've made out. Stage One is 4:08—you should be able to do that by the first week in March. Then we tighten up to four minutes—and you'll need to be down to that by May the first *at the latest*. After that we should be getting somewhere. —Here, you two, no loafing! Get on with it."

Hunter shrugged and said to Foley: "What's the last number on your bus ticket?"

"Six."

"Hell, that means continuous relay. We've had it twice this week already."

"Well, have it three times now," grated Jock. He knew the importance of letting chance decide among the half-dozen training alternatives an athlete had. Training was a grind at the best of times; anything to add interest, however feeble.

"Now, Colin, you take this." He groped in his bag and produced a piece of paper pasted on to cardboard; it was inscribed with figures. "It's your Bible, son. And if it doesn't make you a world-beater then nothing will. —Now away with you and have a shower. Don't let yourself get cold."

The first yellow bulb sprang into light in a house beyond

the fence. It was darker now and, he fancied, colder. Foley and Hunter were running down the back straight, with a half-crystallised mist clinging round them. They were chasing each other endlessly, fruitlessly: one would sprint past the other, then slow down and allow himself to be distanced in turn. This they would do for fifteen minutes, wringing the last drops of physical energy from themselves, beating the body into subjection for another day, until the time came to taper off with gentle jogging, walking and light exercise. But Colin knew Brendan Foley: he would be out tonight on the sharp gradients of the roads that climb Divis and the Black Mountain. Even Rex might stay on in Cherryvale for a few practice starts.

Jock called after him: "Enjoy your dinner!" His gorge rose: the worst cross the runner has to bear is the throwing of his stomach into tumult. He would not eat a bite until the morning.

III

Sitting full of aches in his armchair that evening, he examined Jock's schedule; this, he thought grimly, is going to make my life a misery all summer. The paper read:

110 yds	220 yds	440 yds	880 yds	3/4 ml	1 ml
15.5	31	62	2:04	3:06	4:08
15	30	60	2:00	3:00	4:00
14	28	58	1:56	2:54	3:52
12.5	25	50	1:52	2:48	
12	24	48	1:48		
11.5	23	46			
11	22				
10.5					

At first sight a jumble of figures; but, quickly emerging from it, the three mile times to the extreme right—the steps of his putative progress, 4.08, 4:00 and 3:52. Whatever the other numbers meant they were subservient to these.

Suddenly despondent, Warnock let his hand drop on to the arm of the chair. It was all too complicated; he hadn't energy enough for the effort of interpretation. His throbbing body squeezed rhythmically at its nerve centres. God, but he was tired!

But the invading soreness was worse than the effort of thinking. He raised the hand again, in self defence: perhaps this damned thing would take his mind off his aches and pains.

Let's see then: first line across. Why, it was mere multiplication, each figure twice the one before—signposts for a running machine! The furlong in 31, a lap in 62, half-mile in 2:04. Admittedly the final figure—4:08 for the mile—was what he was aiming at in three weeks' time; but who ever ran as mechanically as that?

The second line, for the mile in four minutes, was even more pointless. He thought back to the first time he had done it himself, eighteen months ago; he was as even-paced a runner as any but his lap times had been 58, 59.7, 62.1 and 58.2, giving a grand total of three minutes and fifty-eight seconds. He thought ruefully: I haven't been able to better that since. But this wasn't the time for self-pity; he brushed it aside. Still, the figures were clearly Utopian.

He thought back again: when I was in training for that four-minute attempt . . . And remembered: I was doing sixty-second quarters, eight in a row with a minute between each. If he had been doing two-twenties there would have been sixteen, each of thirty seconds. Interval training worked that way: twice the actual distance, run over fractions of the course at the same actual rate. So the intermediate figures as you read across represented the targets for interval work if you were aiming at the final figure.

But every miler knew that; it was old hat. What was the point of writing it down? Jock, he knew, wasn't prone to practical jokes, so it must *have* a point.

The figures wriggled on the paper in front of him. He focussed hard on them, trying to make them say something, but they remained mere strokes from Jock's precise pen. Then he noticed the blank space on the bottom right. It cried out to be filled—if Colin had a ruler he would instinctively have drawn a right-angled triangle in it, with the rising line of figures as hypotenuse . . .

Of course, the hypotenuse! What a fool he was; you could also read the figures along the hypotenuse line, diagonally. And that would give you . . .? Well, why not the figure you should be *capable* of, in a once-off performance, at the shorter distance? That must be it.

He followed the diagonal downwards and left from the underlined 3:52, and was dashed. Forty-six seconds for the quarter! That was futuristic, surely. He must have misunderstood. He abandoned that particular line and started from 4:00—a time he had actually done. Let's see if that's more realistic.

It read:

$$2:54$$
$$1:52$$
$$48$$
$$23$$
$$11$$

Haven't ever had a time trial over three quarters of a mile, so I can't judge the last one. But 1:52 for the half—why, I've done that when I beat Foley last summer at Paisley Park! Damned pleased with myself when I did, too.

But a quarter in 48—never. Been inside 49 a couple of times, mind you, so let's say it's on. But 23 seconds for the furlong is really scooting, and as for 110 yards in eleven flat. . .!

Still, we're within the bounds of possibility for the higher figures—if only just.

But moving down to that final diagonal was like a cold douche. The half-mile in 1:48 was two whole seconds better than his best ever time, and 46 for the quarter was well inside the Irish record. Madness.

He took the paper between the index and middle fingers of his right hand and spun it away from himself. It skimmed down to rest on the far corner of the carpet and lay there, a remorseless white splash.

It held his thoughts prisoner. Why, he asked himself, did I feel reasonably at home with that four-minute diagonal? Because it consists of times I've either done or am capable of. Indeed they were times you *had* to be capable of to run the mile in four minutes. He remembered something Jock had once said: "In modern middle-distance running the segments of the race are as important as the race itself." The secret of success at a mile was excellence at the intermediate distances.

So he was back with the impossible again. Raising himself gingerly from his chair, he walked across to where the card lay on the carpet, one edge touching the leopard-skin rug, and squatted down to look at that inexorable final line:

$$
\begin{array}{c}
\underline{3:52}\\
2:48\\
1:48\\
46\\
22\\
10.5
\end{array}
$$

Impossible figures, of course; but, if he was interpreting Jock aright, he couldn't allow himself to think of them as such. They were *not* impossible. Nothing that *has* to be done is.

All the same . . . One forty-eight for the half was just about feasible; you could argue that a world-class miler ought to be able to pull himself down to that time at the shorter distance.

There was no real sense of alienation here. But what a gulf yawned between that and the number below!

Forty-six seconds for the quarter (no point in looking any further, the two sprint times were simply beyond him, should he train till his body was pulp). What *is* my best quarter? Just under forty-nine. And Rex?—But damn it, why bring in Rex? The European record is forty-five—one second less than I'm expected to do. Can I seriously hope to hold the European record-holder to a lead of one second, namely ten yards?

Can Rex even? Hunter's name kept pushing itself forward; this was, after all, his territory. The plain fact was that Rex had never done forty-six flat. No Irishman ever had. But Colin had to! Colin had to beat the Irish record and Rex into the bargain.

Why, for God's sake? His mind rebelled against the idea. The quarter wasn't his distance. He was a miler: four quarters one after the other. Each would have to be fifty-eight seconds, but there was some difference between fifty-eight and forty-six.

Then he remembered Santry, and Horvath: Horvath against whom he had tied up. He remembered trying to force a sprint from himself, a sprint that wouldn't come. Of course! That was what the schedule was designed to remedy. The creation of sustained speed, so that you were able to fall into the quarter-miler's rhythm over that last killing lap.

Again Jock had said it: since four minutes was first beaten the philosophy of miling had changed. It was fruitless now to grope desperately for a last kick, because when you had got within fifty yards of the line you ought not to possess one: you ought to be sliding downhill to the tape, your battle won, remembered strength holding you upright by a thread. And even if things didn't work out that way, even if the pace was slow, you must have the strength to crush opposition over every yard of the last four hundred and forty. You must be moving too fast to kick.

In either case, he was back with forty-six seconds and the need to beat Rex.

He shook his head. How the devil *did* you beat a quarter-miler, a man who ran in one long swoop from start to finish at a pace you had never before attempted? A man who seemingly had no weak point, no momentary slackening of tempo when you could deliver your challenge? It was all very well knowing what you had to do; how the hell did you actually do it? Well, Jock had given the answer to that one too; *he* would provide the system. He would let it rest with Jock.

But he was filled with a new respect for the schedule. It was a clever thing after all, an intelligent system of incentives. Do a forty-six quarter, it said, and I'll give you a world-class mile. Psychologically too it was a winner: Colin could imagine the absurd sense of liberation which a body, trained to forty-six, must feel when asked for as little as fifty-eight. It would be child's play, an anticlimax almost.

He looked again at his magic line. The times for the sprints began to have a meaning now. Not a literal one; they no longer asked him to make himself a sprinter of European class. They said: "Get as close to me as you can." They were bait to make him into a better runner than he conceived himself to be. But the forty-six for the quarter *was* literal; no question of that. The four and the six as he looked at them were hard-edged as steel. On impulse he took the paper into the study and laid it down on his father's desk. There was a writing pad there, and on it he rearranged the figures for his own use:

3:52

46

22   1:48

10.5   2:48

That was more like it; the proportions were right now. To make it even more obvious he ringed the 46 in ink. That very gesture set him in opposition to Rex; he was surprised to discover in himself a certain truculence, as though Rex were physically standing in his way.

IV

The next afternoon he was a mass of stiffened muscle but hobbled out on to the track nevertheless, darkly determined.

"None o' yesterday's bravado, mind," said Jock. "I dinna want to see you rupture yoursel'."

He forced himself through eight two-twenties; the discomfort was acute. "Walk and jog," said Jock. "Always keep moving."

He walked wide round the track, out of the others' way. Foley as he passed smiled reassuringly; Rex let out a wordless shout that roused involuntary guilt feelings in Warnock: this amiable idiot didn't know what was going to hit him.

It rained and they splashed through it, happily.

Next day, Jock examined his notebook and said: "Half miles today. Three of them. Interval: two minutes."

Hunter hated half miles. "What's the use, Jock? I'm a four-forty man, I don't need stamina."

"You may not have wakened up to the fact, Rex," Jock observed drily, "but overdistance makes your event seem easier. Not to mention improving your ventilation. You get two things for the price of one, which ought to appeal to your mercenary wee Ulster soul."

Colin was pleased, for precisely the wrong reason. He chided himself: I ought to be looking forward to shorter stuff than this. Foley, as usual, ventured no comment.

Colin managed all three halves that day but the following afternoon, when the others ran sixteen two-twenties, he could get through only twelve. It was easy to see how they had bene-fitted from those repeated brief efforts of interval training which he lacked.

However in two days, with most of the acid pressed out of his system, he was able to follow the full programme, except for the individual period. Jock nodded to him and said: "You're doing fine, laddie."

"I'm done in, that's what I am."

Jock intoned his favourite quotation. "One of the main charms of interval running is its flexibility . . ."

"Charms!"

Colin did deep breathing and toe-touching while the others were at their individual work. The final number on Foley's bus ticket had again determined it: odd distance. Another look at the ticket—this time at its first number—determined what that distance would be.

"It's a three."

Three hundred yards; that pleased Rex, but Foley gave a small agonised grin. The first number on Rex's ticket decided the next odd distance: six hundred yards. Hunter threw the ticket away in disgust, but was put in good humour again next time round: the second number on Foley's was a two.

Watching Colin swing his long arms down to punch the damp soil between his toes, Jock was satisfied: the boy had recovered enormously fast from his lay-off. It was partly his life-long habit of walking; but mostly sheer talent. He'll make my fortune yet, he reflected.

In two further days—adding up to one full week after that first afternoon—Colin was on the full schedule again and working at the others's pace. Not that he was as fit as they were; only more gifted.

V

"Pace. Pace. Pace. You've got to be able to judge pace." Jock punctuated his words with stabs of the lower arm, his pointed forefinger shooting out at them accusingly.

So they did endless relays, each taking a lap and then handing on the baton. The little white stick went round in a perpetual circle, passing from hand to hand. It was an event which always made Jock excited; he would frown mightily at his stop-watch.

"Fifty-eight seconds! Keep the pace down to fifty-eight!" He ran fifty yards alongside Foley himself, waving the watch at him. "Easy, Brendan, for God's sake. Dinna go off with a rush like that."

Rex winked at Colin. "Watch this."

Foley came striding round the top bend and home, Jock gesticulating at him: "Good lad! Just what the doctor ordered." Hunter took the baton from him, running smoothly, exaggeratedly stylish, mimicking a middle-distance man. "Take a look at your man," snorted Jock. Rex's response was a sudden, wild burst.

"Christ almighty, are you stark staring mad? Stop fooling, you big lig!"

But he was not displeased by this elementary horseplay; the sheer back-breaking monotony of training drove them all mad at times. Then Colin did his lap in fifty-eight precisely, and he relaxed.

They stayed on late that day, running in an orange-red sunset blaze that aureoled them with long darting rays, like baroque saints.

Colin thought: in a few days I'll be ready for that 4:08 mile.

VI

Beth, in the hair drier, burrowed into the heart of the electric whine in search of deafness. There was the safety of isolation here, an ostrich-like security. Her head vibrated until she no longer knew where it left off and the sound began.

Her emotions were mechanical, the brain a small whirring dynamo like the one powering this helmet she was in, making it send its flow of hot electric air—air from the Parisian Metro —to envelop her.

Every weekday she was forced into Colin's company. She was studying Modern Languages and he German only, but the non-French half of her work brought them together under the observing eyes of twenty others who *knew*. Beth had an angry self-command when she needed it: she needed it now. She froze him at every hint of approach.

Not that he did approach much. Once, on the stairs, coming down from a tutorial, a babbled "How are you?", making her squirm with embarrassment. One wordless offering of a library book. The question: "Would you like some coffee?" slid out towards her while he was looking at someone else: intention and reality cross-eyed. She did not condescend to answer.

After that he simply avoided her—rotten bastard, afraid she'd make a scene—and paradoxically that was even harder to bear.

The keeping up of appearances was exhausting her: I'm proud, God knows, but why shouldn't I be?—and even away from him, away from the knowing ones, there was the harshest fact to face, the fact that she had lost him. She might rail against him, berate him, damn him for the fool he was, but she wanted him. There was a gap in her life, like a pulled tooth. She kept returning to the empty space, she simply couldn't get used to it.

This diver's suit of steel and hot air offered temporary escape. But when she came out again, ears throbbing, she knew reality would be there again, waiting to be put on with her coat.

She wanted to be fair to everybody concerned but she called the world to witness: had she not been badly treated?

VII

Because he at last finished a session without feeling utterly exhausted Colin decided he wasn't getting enough work to do. "How do you feel about weights?" he asked Jock.

"Suspicious."

"But everybody uses them these days."

"Folderols. Dinna waste your time on them. You know what Lydiard says: if you're a runner, train by running."

"You're a real old reactionary."

"Look, son, if you want to develop a wheen of muscles you don't need, take up weights. But dinna tell me about it."

Colin thought he was wrong but hadn't the nerve to disobey him. So he followed his advice and ran an extra stint in the evening.

It was uncanny, even exalting, to pound along on the shadowy turf at Cherryvale by the light of the stars and the faint blue glimmer from the street lights on the Ravenhill Road.

Second time out, he put his toe in a shallow cavity—they played rugby here too—and sprawled headlong.

Christ, I've twisted my knee! His diaphragm jerked with panic.

He hadn't. It was all his overwrought imagination. But a superstitious dread of Cherryvale at night took hold of him. He drove home without changing.

VIII

"You tied yourself up in a bleddy knot, that's what you did," Jock said. His elbows pointing outwards like umbrella ribs, he dug his fingers into the soft flesh of his paunch and kneaded it reflectively. Colin stood with his head hanging, his lips tacky from drying saliva.

They had just been through a series of quarters at maximum effort and he was full of bottled-up resentment. Hunter seemed more impregnable than ever.

"I could see it from the stand, as clear as day. No wonder you couldna get past that wee Hungarian." The tone was hectoring; what's all this in aid of? Warnock thought resentfully.

"As from today I forbid you to raise your hands above waist level. —Here, Rex!" Hunter loped over to them. "Away to the half-way mark the pair of you, and come round the last bend together. Flat out. And you, Colin, mind you keep those hands low."

"What's he on about?" Rex asked cheerfully as they walked across to the mark.

"Don't ask me. Just let's get on with it."

"All right, keep your hair on. Ready?" He glanced at Warnock with huffy curiosity.

They threw themselves forward, Colin with concentrated rage, giving every ounce of strength he had. He lost.

"No good, no good!" Jock almost bit the words off with his teeth. "Your arms were still too high. Again."

They set off once more, angry with each other. Again Jock wasn't satisfied. "You're like an old grannie knitting!"

He made them run twice more. The last time, when he had finally accepted Warnock's arm position, Hunter won more decisively than before.

"You'll do this every day from now on," Jock growled in his most curmudgeonly voice. "And what the hell have you been up to all this time, Brendan, saying your rosary?"

Foley trotted over obediently.

IX

A privileged band of Honours aspirants was allowed to work in the library stack. The Gothic brick shell of the building was filled by a central honeycomb of books; steel staircases ran obliquely up its sides. Warnock was climbing one of these, his shoes making a small scuffing noise with a hint of metal reverberation.

The rows of volumes were man-made caverns in which occasional dusty figures prowled, snapping on bays of electric bulbs, making his eyes water.

Three flights up, small gangways led to little alcoves, each with table space for four students. Beth sat in one of them, trying to concentrate on French poetry. At her elbow a window like an open rose reached all the way down to the floor; she was high in the eaves of this church-inspired edifice. Through the grimy glass she could see the rain pour down. Students coming in, climbing the staircase with necks craning after an empty space, had an odour of wetness in their clothes; they smelt like returning gun-dogs.

Je devins un opéra fabuleux . . . One of the craning heads belonged to Warnock. The words dissolved on the paper.

In her niche there was no seat free. Immense relief suddenly transformed itself into defiance. She banged her book shut, picked up her handbag and said: "You can come here. I was going anyway."

Heads swivelled; talking was forbidden here, this was the domain of cobwebs and silence.

She pushed past him before he could gather himself for a reply, and walked off: into the rain, she thought, angry with herself but marching down the stairs just the same.

She had brushed against him; they had not been so close since their quarrel. He stood in her still lingering perfume, seeing from the corner of his eye her dark head disappear round a right-angle bend that took her to the ground floor.

"Do you want that seat or not?" An imperious whisper came from someone in a scarf and glasses who was breasting his way up to the alcove in full expectation of occupying it.

Yes, damn it, he did want it; this obtuse, blinking person annoyed him. "Yes, I do want it."

Sitting there in a chair still warm from her, the page in front of him crammed with the formulae of Verner's Law, he realised that the Beth question was still open. Nothing had been resolved between them in either sense. There would be further dealings, he felt sure; he both longed for them and feared them.

Outside, the rain fell with renewed violence. It was strange to be above it watching it drop down past you in untrammelled fall, absolute dead weight obeying an absolute law. There was an illogical sense of freedom about those plunging drifts.

X

He changed to the early morning. It was exhilarating: sometimes the turf was hard with a white frost his running shoe devastated in small irregular patches; the separate glittering grass blades looked so fragile that he unconsciously listened for the tinkle of broken glass.

He ran in the early dawn, when a wintry greyness in the west was the only trace of the coming day, a greyness that slowly lifted to take in the whole sky.

Or else the morning would be warm and the ground soaking underfoot, so that he sank in too far. He actively disliked that but knew that it was good for him. Hard pounding was what he was after, the kind that gives you leg-strength.

So he would unleash himself in powerful rapid bursts on the heavy ground, weaving like a footballer evading tackles, slowing up then breaking into a sudden sprint. He strained forward to meet an invisible resistance, keeping his body low, hugging the ground as though to prevent an opponent catching hold of him.

Such running could develop into a frenzy; once he found himself darting light-headedly about, switching direction like one of those mechanical toys which turn off abruptly when they meet an obstacle, at the will of his own strength. He had once seen a young dog behave like that in newly fallen snow, the first of winter.

All this happened between seven and eight in the morning, while the lights were being switched on one by one in the brick houses and respectable citizens were wakening to the lunacy being perpetrated on their doorsteps.

XI

The glimmering white hand slid across, cupped itself artfully and squeezed Beth's breast.

She, her head on the man's shoulder and her thoughts

heaven knew where, nuzzled up automatically and kissed his ear. Discreet brilliantine replaced the smell of tweeds.

He squeezed again, more masterfully.

The first erotic irritation of the gland prodded her into awareness; she moved the offending member down to her waist. He whispered "Darling!" as though above mere sexual considerations.

He was a junior lecturer from one of the medical departments whom she had met at a party. Now his car was drawn up on a deserted hard-sand beach, while they watched the sea breaking in white rifts under the moon.

She thought: how did I manage to get here? He tried her groin.

"No, Derek."

"All right. If that's the way you want it."

"That's the way I want it."

They spoke for a moment about the beauty of the scene, by which time he had worked up to her breast again.

"Be sensible now . . ."

A deluge of words came tumbling from him. "Oh Beth dearest just let me if you only knew I swear to God I won't take advantage . . ." The flow was cut short by the contact of his squirming sea-anemone mouth with the side of her face. The hand pressed harder home.

She dug her elbow decisively into his side and pulled back her cheek. He grunted out half a lungful of air; but the hand was still there, pumping away independently as though squeezing an orange.

They struggled with each other, panting and overhot even in this icy season. At last, in fury, she drew out with her left hand and slapped his face. He folded up, punctured, and the hand fell slackly away. He was a half-hearted rapist after all.

"Drive me home."

As she sat stiff and glowering beside him she was filled with resentment against Warnock. It was *his* fault, his fault entirely! He had shown her satisfaction and then withheld it. She felt no malice towards this nincompoop sitting beside her; he was only trying for what he could get. The deep feelings were reserved for Warnock, stiff-necked bastard with whom she would get even.

Her resentment was the stronger because she knew that if this fool had had any real spunk she would have yielded.

XII

Rex, as captain of the Queen's rugby fifteen, invited him to join them in a Wednesday afternoon training canter. It was possible because Jock had shifted his Wednesday session to the morning; he now had basketball in the afternoon, and his three runners had lecture-free mornings in any case.

Colin ran in passing movements with the backs while the forwards practised scrummaging. Then a game of touch rugby was organised; he was put on the wing.

"Yours, Colin!" The ball came out to him and he made for the corner, poised to pass when touched. He was still poised forty yards later when he crossed the line.

"You're no slowcoach," somebody said.

"You gave me too much space." He shrugged his shoulders modestly at Rex.

"Bloody speed merchant," retorted Hunter.

They played for half an hour: thirty minutes of hard running, full of shattering bursts and desperate chases.

Warnock was now marked by Holmes, the acknowledged

sprinter of the side. Once when he was given the ball Holmes uttered a playful bellow and hurtled towards him, bent on a real tackle. Alarmed, he skipped out of the way and handed the ball on.

"Funk! Pansy runner!"

Colin laughed with him, but Rex was furious. "You head-case!" he shouted. "Have you no sense? He's a miler, not a rugby player. Do you want to set him back a month in his training?"

Warnock, perversely, felt annoyed: who was Rex to start playing the Dutch uncle?

Hunter, oblivious, gave him an affectionate glance. He felt a righteous glow: he had shielded the university's star athlete against this lunatic. It would have been rotten if he'd made him pull a muscle.

XIII

"The greatest expenditure of energy," said Jock portentously, "is in the transition from the state of rest to the state of movement." His three athletes, crouched at their starting blocks, looked up at him from bunched, uncomfortable stances. "If you don't believe me just go to a pigeon loft and keep shooing the birds off their perches. In ten minutes they won't be able to stand, let alone fly."

He fingered the pistol and went on. ""That's why it's important for Brendan and Colin to do as many starts as they can. There's no segment of the race with anything like the energy loss."

By now they could scarcely hold their positions: toes in blocks, one foot fifteen inches behind the other, hands spread so that thumb and forefinger just touched the chalk line.

"Now clap hands," he said. They looked up, unbelieving. "Go on. Clap hands when I say so."

They obeyed. Hunter fell on to his elbows, but Colin and Brendan came down on all fours like elephants settling.

"You see?" cried Jock triumphantly. "Rex is the only one who has any idea of what a starting position is."

"He's practised often enough," said Warnock.

"What were we doing wrong?" enquired Brendan.

"You weren't far enough forward. If I'd really fired that pistol half your energy would have gone into driving you upwards. No good at all. The golden rule is: thrust *forward* and you'll come up of your own accord. Like an aeroplane taking off."

Once again he made them get down and perch perilously over their spread hands. Warnock lost his balance and toppled. "We'll wait for Colin," said Jock with elaborate courtesy.

He fired the pistol. Rex's big body hurtled off in a single kinetic explosion. Warnock and Foley were badly left.

"You see? You see?" chortled Jock. "The old hand knows all about it."

He took Warnock by the upper arm and said sternly: "Don't try to lengthen your stride like that. In starting the only thing that counts is getting one foot past the other. The stride'll lengthen of its own accord. And pump with your arms. The arm brings the opposite knee with it."

Then he slapped Rex on the shoulder and said; "You're a bonny lad at the blocks." Colin was unreasonably annoyed.

"Down again. Let's see some more."

Anger helped; he crouched there in a taut fury and pitched forward when the pistol cracked, bent on threshing forward regardless of where it got him.

To his delight he found himself at Rex's shoulder. Why, this was great! His finest moment since he started training again.

"Don't get cocky," Jock reprimanded him. "You're no four-forty man."

Rex was puzzled by all this. Am I being got at? he wondered in his good-natured way. He'd never had such lavish praise from Jock before; and of all people Colin Warnock seemed to be taking it amiss.

XIV

Sitting in the lecture while the mid-Channel Frenchman droned on, Beth had a vision of the sweat and labour that were Warnock's life. That body whose secret he kept so well under his clothes, that moving complex of bone and muscle, was dedicated now to sterile self-mortification.

She was shaken with the memory of those slim muscles with their discreet power: the deltoids her hands clung to at the most intimate of moments, the hard, flat chest muscles that crushed her deliciously, the tense abdominals, the narrow buttocks . . .

To be denied these! Yet at the same time a contradictory pride in him welled up, a fierce protective love of his boyish earnestness, his need to stand well in his own eyes.

Oh God, this was dreadful . . . She squeezed a handkerchief in her hand and closed her eyes. She didn't know what she felt any more; she only knew that she was being forced to walk through fire. But did fire harden, as they said it did? She didn't want to be hardened. All she wanted, God knew, was to play her woman's role; was that too much to ask?

Apparently it was. It seemed to her that she had further, painful lessons in humility to learn.

XV

The starts, the rugby training, the private morning sessions were peripheral; the hard core was the interval training. To your marks, off! To your marks, off! Ready or not, you had to go through with it.

On the first of March he ran eight successive quarters at sixty-two seconds each and said to Jock: "I want to try that 4:08 mile next time out."

Jock snorted. "One swallow doesna make a summer. Same again tomorrow."

There was no point in protesting. But he made a quiet vow that if the old man persisted in being crusty he would get Foley and Hunter to help him make a secret attempt during one of his morning sessions. That wasn't necessary. Next day he did the steady quarters again. "Well, am I ready or not?" he asked.

"You're ready," said Jock in his mildest voice.

The third of March. Waking up, he pulled back his bedroom curtains and peered out. A dark sky loured back at him: would there be rain or snow, forcing him to call the trial off? His athlete's superstition ran wild. He paid great attention to the order in which he put on his socks and shoes, noting with relief that both socks were right side out. His horoscope in the morning paper was, as usual, gnomic. On his way to lectures he kept his eyes open for black cats and workmen's ladders.

All morning he walked as though the floor might at any moment rear up and wrench his ankle. His belly rumbled: Christ, I'm going to fall ill! He didn't. But he was not reassured. After all he might be knocked down by a passing car or arrested by the police on mistaken identity.

The weather at least held. At half past two he stood appre-

hensively on the starting line with Foley: this was his first serious commitment and he wanted terribly not to fail. But the
matter-of-fact attitude of the others helped him. They made no
bones of the fact that for them this was just a chore.

"Take it steady," said Jock earnestly. "String together four of
your regular quarters and forget everything else. —Ready,
Brendan?"

"When you are."

"Pull him round the first half. Rex'll take over from there."

Doing things in style, Jock had brought along his starting
pistol. One smoky report and they were off.

Warnock fretted: too slow, too damned slow!

No, damn it. Just impatience. Leave the pace to Brendan;
he's a cool one.

As they strode past him Jock called out the stop-watch reading: "Sixty! You're a bit ahead." And only a quarter of the distance run.

Then Colin's head cleared and his sense of pace came back.
Yes, he *was* ahead of the clock, but comfortably so.

First half: two minutes and two seconds. Hunter swung into
his circular progress like a man boarding a moving bus and
towed him in his wake.

"Ease off, Rex! You're too fast." Warnock was taking responsibility for himself now. Rex throttled back unwillingly. They
swung round the always-slightly-paralysed third lap.

"Three-oh-seven!" called Jock at the end of it. "You've been
dawdling!"

"Let's go then," responded Rex. Colin gave an affirmative
nod. They stepped out bravely round the last lap but one.

On the back straight he felt a tightening steel hoop round
his chest. The last bend seemed endless; he took it on his float,
not allowing himself to feel what was happening to him, his
concentration buried somewhere in the organs of the upper

abdomen, quietly holding them in place.

The strong finisher is the man who slows down least, Jock had said. True enough this time anyway. Husbanding his small stock of energy, he made it to the line. As he came past three yards behind Rex he saw the trainers' face: it had a look of doom.

It wasn't doom ; it was concentration. "Four-oh-seven-point-one," he crowed, displaying the dial of his watch. "Nice sensible running."

Colin gave a breathy gasp of pleasure, but was rebuked. "You've dug the foundations. Now build the bleddy house."

XVI

Thinking about Foley: This unassuming person was a physical freak, in the good sense.

Last summer a team of physiological researchers had set up their equipment in the gym for an experiment funded by some American foundation: measuring the circulo-respiratory capacity of different types of athletes. Jock had regarded the whole thing with disfavour: "Experiment, my arse. There's only one instrument for measuring what a man's capable of and that's the eye of an experienced coach."

But his runners were intrigued. They were put on a tread-mill with an uphill gradient of one in ten, with a simple brief: run till you drop.

One by one they had ascended that endless hill until they could ascend no more; even when supported under the armpits they slumped forward in a sudden blackout.

Colin did well, but not as well as Foley. With eyes blank in his hawk-like face, he had run through all barriers until his blood gave a momentary acidic reaction: the verge of chemical change. No Irish athlete had ever done that before.

Jock scoffed. "I could have told them that before they started. Brendan's a running machine. If he had your body, Colin, nobody in the world could touch him."

Colin felt the arid breath of austerity on his cheek, the perverse voluptuousness of ascetic surrender. In his own less complete way he worshipped at the same altar; Brendan and he were fellow acolytes.

He reflected on the dividing line there was for runners somewhere between the four-forty and the half mile; Rex simply belonged to a different species. His event didn't require the self-immolation that Brendan's and his did; it didn't demand the protracted driving of the body up to and beyond the bounds of pain. He could afford to be relaxed and human in a way in which they could not.

For example there were his rugby practices, when he didn't turn up for athletics at all. To Colin these seemed the height of self-indulgence: the effort was less concentrated and you could go home feeling happy if you had made a score or brought off a good tackle. But no satisfaction came home with you from athletics training, except the masochistic kind favoured by anchorites and desert fathers.

Again, even when Rex was with them he had less work to do than Brendan and himself. While they were sweating round the track he might be practising his starts, tinkering endlessly with blocks and mallet, sweeping away casual grass blades, hunching down like some hairless ape to explode away on a signal from Jock.

Those starts: Colin was catching on to the technique now. He was staying with Rex: a foot or so behind admittedly, but definitely worrying him.

But that was far from beating him.

He shook his head wearily: would he ever be able to do that? A good start helped of course, but it didn't answer the vital question: where was Rex vulnerable? Colin suspected that Jock knew the answer but wasn't letting on; he preferred Warnock to find out for himself.

XVII

Jock devised a new method for speeding up Colin's stride. One afternoon they arrived at the pavilion to find him immersed in the dust of an old store-room. He emerged carrying six ancient relics: old low hurdles, thirty inches high. They looked at him in blank amazement.

"You kids think you know everything," he said. "Well then, tell me what these are."

"Hurdles," said Rex carelessly.

"Hurdles for what?"

"Pygmies."

"Ach, you know damn all about them. You've never as much as heard about the old two-twenty low hurdles. There was a race for you! They still run it here and there in the States."

They looked at the wooden laths as they would have looked at the plunder of an attic: hallowed by age but otherwise uninteresting.

But Jock made them set them up on the hundred yard stretch, ten yards apart with a twenty-five yard clear run at either end. "Right," he said, "let's see you perform."

In no time there were two pairs of bruised shins and a dislocated hurdle.

"It's damned hard getting over these things," complained Hunter. "I can't work out how many strides to take between them."

"You will when I've finished with you."

The repeated little leaps caught them all in the calf muscles; Colin rubbed his legs ruefully. But they kept doggedly at it. Foley was the first to feel at home with the things; in two days he was stepping over them as if they didn't exist.

Next day, Jock changed the course and made them run in a tight circle with the obstacles twelve yards apart.

"What do you think we are?" shouted Rex. "Bloody circus ponies?" He cupped his hands to make his voice sound like a trombone and intoned *Over The Waves*.

The changed interval upset them badly; their reflexes had been conditioned to the shorter distance. They ran round with mincing steps.

Even Foley sighed. "Why do you make us do this, Jock?"

"Because you hate it."

But they soon found themselves developing more flexible strides, clearing the wooden slats without losing pace whatever the distance between them.

XVIII

The boys still eyed Beth with professional interest, going over her points with the detached air of horse dealers. Figure: excellent from what was visible, but they would have liked a look under that skirt. Breasts: definitely alpha plus; the informed regarded this as her one truly classic feature.

Face: good but too short; jaw line too square. But, in the words of Confucius, who looks at the mantelpiece while he's poking the fire?

Unfortunately there was this Warnock business, which was keeping her out of circulation. Against all the rules, and there being such a scarcity of talent.

Anyway she was definitely going off. That provocative mettlesomeness which scores so highly in such assessments was on the decline; the girl looked positively thoughtful these days.

And the boys were anti-thought.

On principle.

XIX

In his craving for punishment Colin replaced his morning session with evening road-work. When it came to sheer back-breaking effort there was nothing to beat running on hilly roads.

He took a light meal at six o'clock and drove his car through the yellow-lighted city dark over Sandy Row to a street of blackened brick houses off the Falls Road to pick up Brendan Foley. Then they went straight across town to the Castlereagh hills.

He parked the car in a neglected lane he had noted in one of his walks with Beth; they took off their track suits and stepped out to cover the asphalt miles in tennis shoes.

In spite of their cross-country training Colin still found it painful at the beginning; the jarring of his heels on the macadam made his muscles ache. But, he thought with thinly pursed lips, this is doing me good.

They usually ran a three mile stretch, specially chosen for the steepness of its gradients, then turned and ran back: six miles of steady pounding, because it was a point of honour with them never to slacken pace however steep the hill. The crazy toil of ascent and descent sent their hearts hammering and pressed out the sweat on their bodies.

There were two rewards: the satisfaction of having reached a summit, any summit, and—occasionally—what was to be seen from it. One particular hill, a long winding brae rising steadily for a mile, countered their exhaustion with a full view of the city.

On a clear evening the great raft of masonry floated in the glow of its lights, anchored in the channel between the Antrim plateau and the hills on which they ran, stretching up the Lagan valley till it petered out in haze to the south-west. Where it met the sea it was shorn off in a strange geometric outline of docks and slipways. The whole mass, as if gently vibrating, threw up a tremulous orange glow; it was their city and it lay beneath them like a prize.

There were inconveniences too, the worst being the head-lights of cars. These had once been rural lanes with hardly a trickle of traffic, but now progress was piling them up with detached villas, Keep Left signs and electricity transformers. It wouldn't be long, Colin reflected, before athletes like himself would have to go out as far as Comber or Saintfield to find somewhere to run.

There were the other pedestrians too: courting couples who shouted: "Do they pay you for doing that?" or "Take a bus— it's quicker!" For the first few hundred yards this was embarrassing, but afterwards they hardly noticed; with the spending of energy they withdrew deeper and deeper into their own physical suffering and aspiration. They had nothing left for the outside world.

When the long grind was over they got back in the car and drove wordlessly to the Students' Union. There, in the basement, were old high-sided baths and water at boiling point: it hissed as it left the taps. Cradled in two of these, caved in like collapsed bladders, they let the heat do its curative work. Very little was said: who had the energy to talk? They simply lay there while steam curled in wisps from the surface of the water and rose in little puffy clouds when they moved.

Occasionally someone would come clattering down into this cavernous place in search of the lavatories, bouncing echoes off the high ceiling.

The bath left them limp and relaxed. Colin took Brendan home, then turned the car's head towards Balmoral Avenue, letting it drive itself.

He was home by ten o'clock at the latest. Once in bed, he plunged down the steep incline to sleep with a crash. Sleep was a ten hour blackout: no dreams, no nagging preoccupations. This was the realm of the body, and the body exacted unreserved submission.

XX

"Take your shoes off, all of you."

They looked at Jock in comic enquiry. What next? they wondered. The old man was excelling himself this season.

"Go on, get them off."

They obeyed.

"My, you've got pretty toes," said Rex to Brendan in a fairy voice.

"Now," said Jock in his most deadpan voice, "we're going to get back to nature in the raw."

"See what I mean?" lisped Rex.

Jock threw a mute glance heavenwards and went on: "The trouble nowadays is that we've all lost touch with the things that give us animal satisfaction"—he quelled Hunter with a glare—"things that our grandfathers took for granted. The smell of the earth behind the plough. Cow dung. The feel of an axe in your hand. A horse between your legs. —Mind you, being born and brought up in the Gorbals, I missed them too."

He glanced round their small semi-circle. They weren't paying much attention; they got plenty of lectures.

"The point is: this happens in sport too. In a stadium you're cut off from the world outside. Even your feet never touch real ground—you've got spikes between."

Ah, they thought, now we're getting somewhere.

"You're going to do some barefoot running now. You'll understand why when you start."

He made them go round the track two at a time in an endless overtaking game, lap after lap, with the third man always resting out. Colin was astonished to find what a sense of satisfied aggression it gave him to stride past his man with the crisp turf damp between his toes.

Rex clearly felt the same; he sprinted powerfully away from Colin. By God, he's not going to get away with that! Warnock gritted his teeth and set off after him, pressing with every ounce of his strength. Jock's eyes, observing him, narrowed under their hooded brows.

Half way round the top bend, with a hundred and fifty yards to go, Colin realised that Rex was giving everything he had. And *he* was still with him!

They kept up the mad pace through the bend and into the straight; the gap between them remained the same. Colin was fighting exhaustion tooth and nail, but he was still there. Then suddenly, twenty yards from the end of the lap, Hunter eased up. His own willpower flopped in sympathy; they coasted home almost together.

Nothing was said; the session continued. But Warnock was in a turmoil. There wasn't a vestige of proof, but he was convinced that Rex's sudden slackening off was a token of weakness: he had had enough.

"You're like bleddy fighting cocks," said Jock mildly as he passed. Rex, his stint over, stood taking in great gulps of air. He and Foley went on with the pointless game.

When they finished the soles of their feet were stained green.

XXI

The long rows of boxwood cabinets contained drawers full of reference cards, each fitted with a brass handle like a pouting lower lip: these were the abstracts of the dessicated books, piled up like them in symmetrical structures.

Beth was looking for a critical work on Rimbaud, under R because she could not remember the writer's name. The poet had inspired a whole library of his own, through which she made her slow way.

Ah, here it was. Holding back the card with the forefinger of her left hand, she jotted down the reference number, pushed the drawer home and glanced up automatically as a shadow formed itself beside her. It was Colin Warnock.

He gave a tentative smile that glided off from her face to the slip of paper with its long combination of letters and figures. "Did you get what you wanted?"

"Yes."

Conversational possibilities were suddenly exhausted. She was looking fixedly at a spot somewhere in front of his chest.

He forced out, a difficult inspiration: "How are things with you these days?"

"Much as usual," she said, the words sounding like the result of a long struggle for truth. "Very quiet." Then, remembering a certain white hand, she flushed pink.

He didn't notice. Looking into the middle distance, he went on: "I—I'm not doing much either. Just running."

Why were there no reproaches? He had nerved himself for harsh words but there were none coming; she seemed, inexplicably, on the defensive. He was nonplussed.

"Have you done Schuhmacher's essay?" she got out.

"Half finished. Hölderlin's a hard man to pin down."

"For us, not for you. You're bilingual."

"Not completely. Nobody ever is."

The spurt of talk petered out. Her old impatience cocked its head; she was on the point of telling him: for God's sake say something; but her nerve failed. Instead, she said: "Are you going anywhere for Easter?"

"I can't. Training. Mother has an important premiere in Hamburg and wants me to come. But it's just not possible." All this was empty, pure non-communication, but he felt compelled to go on. He said: "How about you?"

"Just home. Maybe to Donegal for a day or two. Daddy has fishing cronies there."

"I've never been to Donegal. There's never been time."

Never been time indeed! What nonsense. Once again she felt the pain of being cast aside for an idea. If only it had been another woman; you could do something with another woman. But what weapons were there against an idea? Her rebellion collapsed, broken-backed.

Like a man, he had noticed nothing. He was standing there with one index finger hooked under the brass tongue of a drawer, pushing in and out the obliquely tilted load of cards.

The sheer gaucheness of it melted her.

Forming the words slowly, he said; "You know, Beth, it's not because I don't . . ." His voice trailed off.

She was silent, gathering her strength, recognising that an important test was coming.

"I mean, feelings don't come into it. There's no need for us not to be friends, is there?"

She shook her head. If she made a move now, touched his hand even, he would be hers; she knew that. But only for a while. The test was *not* to make a move. In the long term, everything depended on not committing him.

He smiled awkwardly. She managed to keep the emotion of the moment out of her face. "My book," she whispered, indicating the slip of paper clutched in her hand.

"Of course."

She pushed her way through the door into the book stack, leaving him. He walked out into the cold air of March, oddly elated but with a dangerous corner of his mind sealing itself off.

In the stack, Beth leaned her forehead against the cool metal of a shelf support. It was dark in there, and she was thankful. Thankful too that in his man's way he had only an imprecise knowledge of his own feelings. He had blundered through the danger without really being aware of it.

Thankful most of all for the victory she had won over herself. Surely now, with the gift of patience, she might win?

XXII

Time wore on. At a certain level of intensity physical effort is drained of reality and becomes a symbol; Warnock was embedding himself deeper and deeper in this symbol when a sudden interruption threw him into a panic of alienation.

They were running a crippling series of two-twenties round one half of the Cherryvale track when the dense black sky overhead began to snow on them: moist, heavy flakes that slapped on to the wet ground and seemed destined to melt at once. Only the thickness of their fall preserved them.

But night brought one of March's unpleasant surprises, a hard frost that locked the ground in a congee of frozen slush glazed over with ice. The streets were long avenues of grey scurf with narrow white edgings, the roads impassable. It was the last day of the Hilary term.

Track work was impossible; Colin spent all morning playing badminton with Hunter in the gym. Then Jock arrived, well aware of the fact that his athletes would be there.

Colin was worried; training had become a needed drug. "What can we do?"

"Aagh." Jock emitted a long moan of annoyance and looked across to a corner of the hall where there was a black gleam of metal. "Nothing for it. You'll have to use them bleddy things till the frost clears."

Weights at last. Colin could hardly believe that the old man was yielding; last year when it snowed he had invented indoor exercises for them. Clearly he had been reading the specialist press; every day, it seemed, there was a new story of some top runner going over to weights.

They walked across to a collection of bar-bells and dumb-bells that made Colin think, inconsequentially, of railway bogeys. "No overdoing it, mind you," grated Jock, trying to reassert his questioned authority.

He chose three exercises for them, one for arm-drive, one to strengthen the quadriceps above the knee and one for the chest.

Twin steel rods ran vertically up the gymnasium wall; on

them slid, graphite-lubricated, a pair of fifteen-pound cast- iron blocks. Ropes ran from the top surfaces of these, via pulleys at waist level, to hand grips like leather stirrups. You posted yourself facing the wall, far enough back to hold the weights a foot from the floor; the ropes twanged taut before you. Then you started punching: left hand, right hand, left hand , right hand, as fast as you could; it was the sprinter's arm action only the palms of the hands were downwards. The object was speed, speed, speed. You snatched the rope back, the weight carried it forward again, you snatched once more. Yes, it was like sprinting all right, but gravity had added fifteen pounds weight to each arm.

The dumbbells were simple iron discs mounted on twelve-inch axles as thick as a crowbar. Their rough black surface was mottled here and there with rust, and each disc was held in place by a washer-nut painted with a dab of red. Hunter was tempted to send them rolling across the precious maple floor, just to hear the rumble.

But he refrained and, like the others, lay on his back on a low bench, legs astride, feet resting on the ground. Jock had set the dumbbell on its end on the floor behind his head; he reached backwards and downwards, heaved its thirty pounds up till it dangled in the air above his staring eyes, then slowly let it fall back. Thirty times he did that, till his armpits ached. This exercise developed the chest.

To strengthen the thighs they had bench-stepping.

"Do you mean the Harvard test?" asked Foley modestly.

"Clever laddie," said Jock with sarcasm. "Been at the books agin."

"What's the Harvard test?" asked Rex.

"Och, nothing much. You just step up on tae a bench and back down again. Only you've got an extra ten pounds to carry. — But you're no doing it the day; you've had enough."

He was right. Ten minutes struggling against the resistance of a dead weight had broken them.

XXIII

The ten pounds were worn in a leather belt round your waist, like false money. Foley quoted an article from an athletics magazine: *three minutes of this exercise exhaust the average man.*

"Three minutes hell," said Rex; he was no average man. Colin quietly determined to do it for five.

"Anybody got a watch?" Jock asked with an innocent look. "You need to time yourselves, don't you?"

As he well knew, they had left their wrist watches in the changing room. So he produced an odd-looking object from his pocket.

"What the blazes is that?" said Rex.

"An egg timer. It *was* three minutes, wasn't it, Brendan?" Grinning like an old monkey, he attached the device to the wall by its suction cap.

Foley attempted a mild joke. "In the article they did it to a metronome. You wouldn't have one of those on you too?"

"Not one me. But there's one in my office." He rummaged in the other pocket and handed Colin a key.

"For Christ's sake don't make me laugh," protested Hunter. "I'm so stiff from yesterday I'll split down the middle."

When Colin returned with the little wooden pyramid he found an eighteen-inch bench made ready and Foley with the belt round his waist. Jock wound up and set the metronome; the thin brass arm ticked at forty-five beats to the minute.

"Start the timer, Rex. —O.K., Brendan, show us how."

Hunter upended the timer—scaled-down hour glass with its midget lesson of mortality—and the sand began to flow. Foley stepped rhythmically up and down. After three minutes his breath was thick and there were small red circles on his cheeks. He was beginning to stagger.

Rex and Colin had their turns too: the thing looked like nothing much but was a potent devourer of energy. They finished with aching thigh muscles; no question of five minutes this time.

When the short murderous session was over Jock made them relax methodically, limb by limb. Standing on one leg, they would shake the other, willing each separate muscle to go slack until the entire clothing of the bone became one inert, flapping mass. He called this passive massage.

As for the chest, he made them move their shoulders up and down in silent laughter; the slender slabs of breast muscle with their small male paps moved in rhythm.

Next morning, as suddenly as it had come, the frozen slush melted and ran off. In Cherryvale itself the ground soaked it up, but in the street outside it sang in the gutters.

They did no more gym work after that; but Colin made a secret decision to carry on by himself. The sheer pointlessness of exerting yourself against an inert lump of metal had a fascination about it. Besides, he had a superstitious need to embrace every possible variety of training experience. How could he measure himself against competitors who might have wider knowledge than his own?

XXIV

Outdoors again, Jock put them straight on to quarter-miles but disturbed the pattern of the starts. Where, before, the others had been chasing Rex, now Rex chased them.

He was placed in the inside lane, with Foley and Warnock to his right; they were a visible target for him to aim at but had no idea of his position themselves. Not until the final bend was turned and the stagger unwound would the true state of affairs become known.

"Now Rex," said Jock, "make up as much ground as you can. I want to see you in the lead when you come out of that bend."

He turned to the others. "You two won't see him coming. It's up to you to do those three hundred and seventy yards *flat out*. Forget about saving something for the finish; we're not concerned with finishing just now. —No, I'm not telling you *what* we're concerned with, but if you come out of that bend level with Rex you'll have done more than you know."

Colin, remembering the barefoot session on the grass, pricked up his ears: not more than *he* knew. Three hundred and seventy yards, Jock had said. He must drain Rex dry by three hundred and seventy yards. That was the way to the forty-six seconds quarter.

He didn't succeed. Not that day. He had the frustrated feeling of a tennis player who is slightly off form: potentially the strokes are there, but somehow he can't make them come. Perhaps tomorrow . . .

XXV

The deserted quadrangle was bright with April sunshine. He met Schuhmacher coming across it; they spoke of that neglected activity, work.

"I'm sorry about that last essay. It was bad."

"You will do better."

"Time's the problem. Essentially, I only have mornings now. And even then I'm in the gym from twelve."

Schuhmacher smiled. "You have never given yourself wholly

to anything before. It is important that you should."

"I know. But . . ." He was conscious of free-wheeling along, taking the odd note, nothing more. His mind was miles away: other lecturers passed sarcastic remarks when he made a silly answer in a tutorial or woke from a daze to the realisation that he was being asked a question. He felt uncomfortable about it.

"There will be time enough later, when the summer is over."

"No. The Olympics are in December." But Schuhmacher was right. The odd Queen's academic system favoured him. He was a Third Year Honours student: there was no formal examination, merely a small class test, which he could easily pass, at the end of next term. After that: nothing until his finals, in the summer of next year. He had fourteen clear months ahead.

"Even if you compete in the Olympics you will still have six months for work. With your background that is enough."

It was true; he was free to run. And now, in vacation time, with no lectures or essays to distract him, that freedom was total. He could withdraw completely into the narrow world of his choice, as though behind the steel curtain of a jeweller's window. Nothing and nobody could touch him.

Thank God for the financial independence that allowed him to follow this stubborn path of his towards self-realisation: his father had at least done that for him, had caused the disease perhaps but provided the antidote as well.

He thought of Brendan Foley, the eldest of a family of nine: he had to take spare-time work to help his parents out, and study hard as well. Failure at his dentistry could not be contemplated; like death, he could not allow it to enter into his calculations.

Could I do what Foley is doing in his circumstances? He doubted it. The supreme realisation he sought would perhaps always be a luxury, could not be anything else.

In the four-forties he felt himself trembling on the verge of a breakthrough.

XXVI

Easter had slid silently past. The regular routine made time non-existent; a day had gone by before you really knew it. It was near the end of April.

The four-minute mile by May the first, at the latest: that was what Jock had said. Well, he was ready. In interval training he was doing his eight quarters in a fraction under sixty seconds. There was in him a stock of pent-up energy, laboriously created. That, and the sense of having his muscles filed to an ever sharper edge of fitness without there being anything for them to cut into, made him clamour for the time trial.

"How about doing that four minutes tomorrow?" he said to Jock.

The Scot looked at him critically—he was sure the answer was going to be no—than said: "O.K. But not over the distance. Let's see just how strong you are: you'll do two miles instead."

"For God's sake! I'm sick of running every distance except my own. I want a genuine test."

"You think overdistance isn't genuine?—No, Colin, I'm your trainer and I say no. Psychologically it's out of the question. If you miss the four minutes now it'll set you back weeks. No more miles for you, laddie, till July."

Colin protested. There was an argument, after which they compromised on a mile and a quarter; it was the closest Jock would go to his real distance. Pulling a dog-eared booklet from his pocket, he announced: "Five minutes and ten seconds: that's the equivalent of four minutes for the mile."

Brendan and Rex pulled him home in a fraction over 5:09. Jock was secretly delighted, but deflated Warnock, eager for congratulation, with a curt remark: "Aye. Fine. Now let's get down to the serious stuff."

Praise was a currency. Devalue it now, and what would he have for money when the lad really did turn in something special?

XXVII

Warnock tingled as he crouched at his blocks, yards ahead of Hunter, yards behind Foley; he had the middle lane of the three. After yesterday's time trial he felt good.

On Jock's signal they leapt away from their wooden wedges and hurtled round the first bend, flat out. Colin thought, grimly exultant: I am going to run this pair into the ground. To maximise speed he pretended that the race would finish at the end of the back straight; only when he had flown past that mark did he brace his muscles for the next stretch.

This was the vital time: he could see that he had closed the stagger on Foley by maybe two yards—but Hunter? Couldn't begin to guess. It would be fatal to look round, you lost impetus that way. Trust to that feeling of absolute performance your body ached with.

He drove himself round the last bend, aware of trailing Hunter by a thin cord from his heels. He must break that cord. Whatever the cost.

As he watched them straighten out for the run-in Jock's eyes widened: Warnock was ahead! How much? A yard—no two, even three!

Was this it? Or was Rex hanging back, saving himself for a last burst? His hand holding the watch trembled; his wits weren't working fast enough to calculate whether it was a good time or not. But he had an impression of fast, unbearably fast movement.

Now Hunter was making his effort. He saw the big fellow

gather himself, thirty yards from home, but he could go no faster; he was drained, dry. Colin had squeezed the energy from him in that fourth hundred.

"Forty-six point four!" Jock shouted, waving his hairy arms. Rex flung disconsolately past, three yards behind Warnock; Foley was five behind that. The odd thing was that they had all three chosen to do their best times at this killing distance on the same day. Colin and Rex were inside the Irish record (held by Rex).

By an act of will Jock sobered himself. "Enough of the high jinks! Jog a lap."

"Damn the jog!" Hunter was purple-faced: exhausted but nettled. "We'll have another." He glared at Colin.

"Suits me." Warnock wheezed the words out. "Any time."

"Well it doesna suit me," said Jock coldly. "What do you think you are, prize fighters? No more quarters till Saturday."

"But Saturday's the first meeting of the season."

"Exactly. Against Collegians. Brendan, you'll be doing the mile—and no arguments. Rex, two-twenty and quarter. Colin, quarter and half. You can tussle to your heart's content at Deramore."

He reflected: the graph of progress is a series of plateaux. Was this the beginning of a new one, the most important one yet?

XXVIII

God but it was cold at Deramore! The wind blew with Siberian malice, as though to punish mankind for daring to think of a season of athletics. Colin was frozen to the bone.

In the throes of reaction, he was beaten by Rex in the quarter; his time was 48.2. Somehow he couldn't shake off the numbness of the wind.

In the half, over-anxious to get past his man, he tripped and fell and was lucky to escape spiking. The papers spoke mournfully of his performance.

XXIX

Schuhmacher had invited him to tea the following day. He trained in the morning with a sort of baffled irritation, and drove to the professor's house in the afternoon.

It was May now and, by contrast with yesterday, the hottest day of the year so far. Tiny high fleeces of clouds ran in parallel lines across the sky and there was bright sunshine on the single lime-tree of College Park, molten light that poured through the gaps in its moist, still wrinkled leaves coloured a vulnerable green. He could practically feel those leaves stretch out and unroll themselves; growth was a tangible thing. There was a breeze to keep the foliage in a mild continual stir, constantly sifting it as though discontented with its arrangement.

Schuhmacher lived in a Victorian terrace house of imposing proportions. From his second-storey drawing room the view was over tree-tops at eye level: horse chestnut, Austrian pine and the single lime tree in a receding vista. "The work of generations," he observed elegiacally, looking out with a just arrived, taciturn Warnock at his side. "Generations of growth to produce this effect. One generation more and it will be destroyed." He smiled in self-mockery.

It was a room of books. One wall was shelved to the ceiling and there seemed to be a bookcase tucked away in every available corner. All were full but not overflowing; the contents were neatly arranged, apparently by size and shape rather than by subject.

As for the rest, it was a far warmer, brighter, more comfortable room than one had the right to expect from an ageing bachelor. There was a good Tienstin carpet on the floor, honey-coloured with a simple pattern in green; and he had placed capacious modern armchairs side by side with antiques like the long-legged satinwood cabinet with a cloisonné vase on top or the ottoman upholstered in a velours that was a wondrous match for the green of the carpet. Beside the big window, where it caught the light, was his Louis Seize writing desk, all rosewood veneers and sculptured brass.

His housekeeper brought in tea and cakes in impeccable English style. Warnock, warmed by the drink, said: "I've often wondered: how come your books all look so clean?"

Schuhmacher smiled. "Having no wife, I can at least insist that my bindings be handsome."

"I should have thought you were a man for buying up everything you saw."

"In the old days, yes. Then the only thing that counted was the text. Also I had no money. But little by little I replaced what was ugly."

"Do you never buy cheap books nowadays?"

"On the contrary. Look at those calf-bound Waverleys; I picked them up for a song at a country auction last year. I must confess to having felt sorry for the poor dead owner. Then I reflected: perhaps they needed me as much as I needed them."

They chatted about indifferent things: literature, politics, common friends. For a naturally tense man Schuhmacher expanded here among his fine furniture and expensive bric-a-brac. In deference to Sunday he had exchanged his usual lumpy tweeds for a well-cut grey suit that made his jowl seem less black, almost lent him charm.

"You are lucky being young in the sixties," he said. "The Cold War gives a kind of security; you know where you are in it. Germans who were young in the last years of the Weimar republic, like myself, knew nothing of security. An impotent Reichstag, communists and Nazis clashing in the streets. How can one produce anything of value in such times? I certainly couldn't. —And what followed was even worse."

"Didn't Goethe produce *his* work at a time of national crisis?"

"He was a Titan. We smaller creatures have to scramble up to achievement as best we may. Speaking for myself, I can only do so in peace, and I never had that. Perhaps that is why I am attracted to writers like Nietzsche, whose whole life was turmoil, a constant reaching out to something that constantly withdrew."

"When did you first take an interest in that kind of writing? At school, or later?"

Schuhmacher gave his ironic smile. "Not, as so many academics do, when I discovered an untouched field for research. I did read them at school of course, but I really came to them later, through music. —Can I offer you more tea?"

Schuhmacher poured; the liquid made a shining vortex in the cup. "Did you know that my mother was a distinguished amateur violinist?"

Colin glanced up at a faded photograph on the wall. "All I know about her is that picture."

"She could have been a professional, but we were a bourgeois family. My father played too, although he was a surgeon by profession. And my sister. Even I learned the cello. If I know the Haydn quartets passably well it is because we played so many of them together at home."

"What a talented race you are!" Colin felt rueful admiration; beside this his own background seemed so barbarous. The question was: did he have the compensatory energy?

"We went to the opera practically every week; we had a subscription. I became a fanatical Wagnerian. That is where I acquired my taste for the heroic, the over-inflated even." He paused for a moment, sipping his tea.

"Wagner led directly to Nietzsche, so when I went up to Leipzig university in 1927—I was just nineteen—it was to study both literature and philosophy. You've seen a copy of my doctoral thesis: *Nietzsche's Concept Of The Good Life*. A difficult subject; Nietzsche is a baffling author, like all those who write philosophy in the language of poetry. Though I am inclined to believe that poetry is the only language it *can* be written in."

"You didn't become cynical, like the bright young things of your generation?"

"No. I was rather unworldly, I suppose. I even ignored the Nazis until about 1930; I suppose I couldn't bear to think that they might have a role to play. I didn't fully waken up until 1933, and then it was too late. There was an end to heroic music and literature, and end to writing poems—"

"You wrote poetry? You never told me that."

Schuhmacher's eyes flickered, then he recovered himself. "No. I have never told anyone here in Ireland. And in Germany there are none left to remember."

Warnock felt immense excitement and curiosity. What on earth could a poem by old Klaus be like? He *must* still have copies; authorial vanity would scarcely allow a man to lose every last line, even in a revolution. But he dared not ask. He said: "Were they traditional or experimental?"

Schuhmacher did not answer directly. "They were about the same kind of thing that interests me today: dedication to something above and outside the self. Call it inspiration, call it heroism. Hence the title: *Der Wind Gottes*. The Wind Of God."

"The *title*! You mean they were published? But that's marvellous. I've never met a real live German poet. Do you still write?"

"No," said Schuhmacher curtly. "That is my only published work."

"I'm sorry."

"You need not be. I stopped writing, that is all. The world became too disturbing. It was dangerous for Jews like us to walk in the street. A gang of young Nazis beat up my father and left him for dead; indeed he did die shortly after. —But what is one death beside the deaths of so many?"

"You never told father any of this."

"No honourable man wants to arouse pity. It was bad enough being a refugee without that."

"Pardon my saying so, but I can't help wondering why you didn't turn your back on German culture, on the whole German experience, after that. It's baffling, and rather touching, how so many German Jews cling to their background in spite of everything."

"Can you turn your back on the air you breathe, the language you speak? I left physically of course; I had just become Doktor Schuhmacher so I packed my bag and went to Cambridge—where I had once attended a summer school—to give private lessons, eventually to get a post at the university. But my mind is still in the Leipzig of 1932."

"And your family?"

"All dead. The evening before I left Mother and I had a fierce argument. I wanted to take her with me but she refused to go. My sister too. They said the evil, the madness, would pass in a year of two. They were among the first to be put in a camp. The letters stopped coming in 1937. By that time I had elaborated my thesis for the English doctorate—which, as you know, is more difficult than the German one—and was on the verge of my first appointment as Reader."

He put down his cup with an elegant movement of the

hand. "Then, after the war, Belfast. Your country was then—and is now, I may add—profoundly strange to me. By nationality and race I am doubly a foreigner. And as a Jew, it is too difficult for me to go back to Germany, even if I wanted to. So I stay on, fairly happy, almost enjoying it, but foreign. I have been foreign all my days, it seems, sending down roots but unable to sink them in real soil. When that happens you cannot make very much of your life. Or so at least I have found."

There was so much controlled grief in his voice that Warnock could not say a word. But he understood better than before his own position in Schuhmacher's universe: faced with the chaos of the world, the other man had abdicated ambition and pursued heroism only in books. But he could not prevent his longing for a sort of absolute from breaking out and identifying itself with his, Colin's, running. As for himself, he had a profound sense of his own inadequacy, his inability ever to live up to such expectations.

"But I am boring you with all this. —Let us talk about that last essay of yours . . ."

At five o'clock, as Colin rose to go, the professor said: "Oh by the way, I got wind the other day of a potential biographer for your father. Maxwell from Edinburgh. He hasn't approached you yet but he will. I assume you will say yes, so I have put all Robert's letters together. Will you take them now?"

He produced from his desk a shoe-box tied with red tape. "They're inside, in chronological order, the earlier ones to the bottom. I didn't file them; Maxwell will want to put them in with the other correspondence. The recipient isn't important."

Colin leafed through them when he got home, starting at the top of the pile. That was taking the great man back to front, but for his son it had a certain logic; it was going from the known to the unknown. Robert as Director General of the

United Nations Food and Agriculture Organisation (an apotheosis cut short by the air crash): "Sitting, even in distinguished company, chafes the backside." Robert the academic. Robert the wartime civil servant. Robert in Africa.

There were occasional references to himself: brief, unemotional. "Keep an eye on my boy while I'm away, will you? I seem to get less and less time with him . . ." "How's the athlete of the family?"

Years back, he found a note that began:

> Dear Klaus,
> I can't get my mind off the boy of mine. It stops me concentrating on my work. Does he show any sign of being interested in *anything*? Or am I to be saddled with a good-for-nothing? I don't know what to do about him. Advice please.
> That little runt Jeffries with his Malthusian moanings makes me see red . . .

Anger, hurt and retrospective guilt drove from his mind any thought that Schuhmacher might have planted this as a sort of time bomb, although it could hardly be a coincidence that he had chosen to give it to him the day after he had lost an important race. He could think only of his father: his father's harshness, his father's injustice. Damn him! Damn him!

The anger galvanised him. He would train himself into the ground, mutilate himself, endure any privation, to prove him wrong, to have the last word.

Privations were a currency: you could buy achievement with them.

XXX

As the evenings lengthened Foley and he kept moving back the times of their roadwork. Training was for them a secret process, to be carried out only before initiates. They claimed the athlete's privilege of privacy while he is preparing his appearance: to him the grind of training is as the chipping of stone to a sculptor, something that concerns himself alone. The public has a right to the matured performance, nothing more.

Jock's main preoccupation was teaching them to relax. He said to Warnock: "Every miler has a last reserve of running in him even when he thinks he's exhausted. The trouble is, very few people know how to draw on it. They're tense, they bottle it up. Relaxation's the answer: relax properly and you can give everything. You ought to be keeling over at the precise moment you hit the tape. You'll never do that if you're tense."

But this relaxation had to be combined with speed. To coach them in the fast, smooth release of energy he made them do two-twenties from a moving start.

This was balm to Rex after his humiliation in the four-forty. All three would approach the chalk line abreast, accelerating as they crossed it. After that it was one long burst over the furlong. Rex invariably won; there simply wasn't distance enough to sap his stamina.

Warnock and Foley tore along in a paroxysm of rage, exasperated by constant defeat. Wait till they got this bastard over the half! Even the quarter would do. But they never did. Jock made them run this infuriating distance again and again.

Hunter expanded, became himself again. He would slap them on the back and say: "Not bad, you fellows. You made me stretch that time."

They hated it, but were being toughened mentally without

realising it. And by a process of feedback they became physically stronger too, the hardened psyche lending the body confidence and tone.

XXXI

The Trinity term ended in the middle of May, and classes with it. Not for Schuhmacher the last blind rush to finish the course. He had gauged his material perfectly; he began his peroration ten minutes before the end of the final hour.

Outside, the air was restless with insects, the sky youthfully blue. The girls were in their summer frocks: striped, flower-patterned, short-sleeved man-made blooms. Beth's was of a striking green, splashed with areas of white, the bodice moulding the bosom closely, the skirt flaring out boldly from the waist.

". . . such then was the problem these men set themselves, the well-nigh insoluble problem of reorienting man to his surroundings in a natural way, of vanquishing the self-consciousness that had stifled and poisoned him as ivy stifles a tree, of reinventing God. It defeated Nietzsche and Hölderlin, it drove them mad. Perhaps Kleist too, although his suicide is a hard thing to interpret."

He arranged the words as calmly as if they were counters, thought Colin admiringly; yet they were the distillation of his own dilemma.

Ten feet away, Beth was tossing her black hair impatiently; he sensed her unreasoning antagonism to these sterile strivings, this reaching out to the more-than-human. Crying for the moon, Patricia had called it. But how sterile *was* it, even in

166

the practical sense?

"What solutions had they to offer? Had they *any* solutions? Or is this a problem that can only be stated, not solved? Hölderlin and Nietzsche could answer only by postulating the impossible. We cannot become ancient Greeks again, or supermen. Not in any literal sense.

"Kleist is different. He came to see that we must give up our intellectual pretensions. You cannot attain to unself-consciousness through the intellect. But you can through rediscovery of a state of mind, a state of mind he objectified in the image of the puppet, the will-less object that acts through re-action and is servant of an absolute master: gravity. It thereby achieves grace, a grace shared by the animals, who are also unhampered by conscious will.

"You will say this is begging the question; you can't solve a metaphysical problem in terms of aesthetics. And you would be right. But remember, what Kleist sought in the first place was a natural relationship to the world; perhaps the fault lay in his initial posing of the problem.

"I would also suggest that the puppet, chosen as a symbol, was perhaps even more of a symbol that he realised. It suggests the world of play. Play also sets limits to the individual will: games have rules, their arenas—whether theatres or running tracks—are strictly delineated, they involve the suspension of a thousand factors relevant to our day-to-day life."

He paused for a moment. "I use the word play in its broadest sense: the choice of an activity otherwise pointless, regulated by strict canons, hedged in by obstacles inherent in itself. In short, everything we associate with the abiding pleasures of life: philosophy, science, and all amusements from Nero's circus to the high arts. Especially the arts, I think. In writing of the puppet theatre, Kleist was in my view making the apologia for his poet's trade."

He began methodically to put together his books, his slips of paper, his chalk-box and his spectacles, his pen and pencil, placing them together in a perilous heap on top of his old red register. His students, in expectation of release, slowly expelled their breath. Then, raising one eyebrow, he said:

"So you see it's all very simple. We merely have to discover what the world wants of us and then dedicate ourselves to that. Of course, having discovered that, we are faced with a further problem: *how* to achieve that total dedication. On that point Kleist is unfortunately silent."

He coughed delicately into his hand. "If you should find the answer to that during the vacation your time will be well spent. I should be grateful if you passed the information on to me. And now, till next term, *Auf Wiedersehen*."

They walked out into the sunshine, leaving him to his problem of killing the self-conscious for another year. It was their last lecture and they were loth to separate. They strolled in an untidy knot across the square and under the archway into the quad. It was hot there; the air was trapped inside the rectangle of buildings, above the shaven grass. The Japanese cherries were in rich bud; a day or two would see them bursting into insubstantial blossom.

Their co-evals were scattered about on the macadam and lawns, the fair, chunky youth of the city mingling with darker-skinned students to whom this scene represented the height of the exotic. Beside them on the ground lay piles of heavy notebooks and white-ticketed library tomes. Ask them what they were doing and they would point to these with the single word: "Revising."

The German specialists found a place for themselves and talked about the holidays.

"Where are you going?"

"By freighter to Iceland."

"Koblenz, to my pen friend."

"Nowhere. I'm broke. I'm going to read all of Proust."

"Ten bob says you won't make it."

"Done. I'll take it in stout."

"I'm cycling in the Loire."

"Watch out for the Tour de France. You might win a stage."

"Poor old Colin will be flogging up and down the roads, no doubt." Eyes turned towards him.

"Crafty lad. Angling for a free ticket to the Olympics."

Colin smiled. They admired him, as sportsmen are admired, but they liked making little malicious jokes about him; it helped reassert the superiority of the intellect, as represented by themselves.

He shifted to where Beth was sitting, still smiling to show that he was still of their party. "What about you, Beth?"

"Florence—or rather Fiesole. Somebody gave Daddy the name of a *pension* there: Pensione dei Fiori. It is considered important that I absorb some Renaissance painting." She was not looking at him directly; he saw her face in profile. Her forefinger was tracing the pattern in her green dress.

"Don't miss Siena while you're there. It's not far."

She nodded. They sat in silence for a moment, then someone made a move. The group broke up, reluctantly at first, then with the cheerfulness that a change of place inspires: they were going somewhere, they had an object in view.

Beth got up gracefully and stood haloed by the sun above him. He felt a momentary pang; the months ahead seemed blank and desolate.

He would have said more, but there was no chance. She held out a resolute hand and said: "Cheerio, Colin. See you next term."

His own hand groped out to hers, felt her fingers' pressure. Two more words: Good luck," and she had gone.

XXXII

In a matter of days the faculties had closed down. The university was deserted save for the false teeth makers of Dentistry and a few austere devotees of work, morose fellows who made their way every morning to favoured seats in the library stack. Their schedule is as tight as mine, thought Warnock.

Life narrowed down to the training track and the Saturday meeting, his contacts to athletes: Brendan and Rex in the foreground, further back the other members of the university team —runners, hurlers and leapers whose events formed the three provinces of the athletic world.

Further back still, on the horizon of his life, were their weekly opponents: the Old Boys, belonging to clubs as fashionable as Warnock's own, and the working class teams, rough and ready lads taken from the back streets by organisers whose purpose was as much social as sporting. These boys from the redbrick rows, with docked, bristly hair and old men's faces, scoffed at Colin's sort on principle but admitted these less feckless representatives of their class to a guarded fellowship.

In his solitude his thoughts turned more and more to his body, that instrument which was to propel him over one thousand seven hundred and sixty yards in eight seconds under the four minutes and win him an Amateur Athletic Association championship. The task would not be an easy one; there would be two world-class athletes in the field: Galliver from Oxford University, the European champion, and the great Russell, holder of the Olympic title.

Russell, an Australian, now lived in Cambridge where he was working on a medical doctorate; he belonged to the new wave of athletes, scientists of the body who knew as much about physiology as any specialist.

Jock regarded them with ill-disguised scorn. "Christ Almighty," he would say, "you need to have a bleddy stethoscope to show your neb on a track these days. We'll end up seeing them blowing into wee plastic bags on the way round, to measure their lung capacity or some such balderdash."

Colin had no doctorate, but was becoming a physiologist in his own way. Stretched out in his armchair of an evening, his mind on nothing in particular, he would find his thoughts crystallising.

It started with his legs. They materialised from the void: parallel columns of bone, neatly articulated at the knee and flanked by the outrider fibula; below, the foot, with its sheaves of osseous shafts succeeding each other smaller and smaller like the vertebrae of a young bamboo. These twin pillars, with their rigid cell-structure outside and the warm marrow within, were the key elements without which nothing could be achieved.

But they depended in their turn on a web of muscle and flesh as unique as themselves, a web honeycombed with blood-vessels: arterial tubes splitting off again and again to send their load of energised blood into the ever narrowing capillary system, that tortuous mesh of one-way streets where traffic slowed to a walking pace till, finally, the tiring pedestrians, blue from lack of oxygen, were pushed passively into ever broader thoroughfares, steadily gathering speed and pumped upwards against gravity.

In parallel to this existed the nerves, broad telephone cables throwing off branch after branch until they too petered out; along them hurtled the brain's messages. "Flex the calf!": a lightning call was put through and the muscles, receiving it at their local exchange, pulled themselves together into a fibrous ball, drawing strength from the oxygen the capillaries fed to them.

Those muscles: they were the positive leaven, autocrats who, when they elected to move, dragged everyone else with

171

them.

But they had the obligations of the autocrat too; they drove themselves on and on until excess of acid sent shooting agonies through them, beyond the threshold of pain until the obligations were met in full.

Above the legs was the abdominal wall, so often the traitor with its spectacular cramps or insistent, biting stitches. Then the heart, tireless leather pump sucking in the exhausted blood and spurting it out lungwards in a single movement.

The lungs: strong rubbery sponges filled and voided alternately by the diaphragm, where the blood and outside air were brought into seething contact: the body's power station, rejuvenating the exhausted cells and sending them careering off down the aorta or up to the head and arms, fretted with small crazy air-bubbles, brilliant red with the life essence and galloping to the body's extremities like unbroken colts.

There was more than a whiff of mysticism in this corporeal meditation; a wind of voluptuous asceticism blew over him. He did not so much perceive his body as commune with it.

And day by day it went through its scheduled punishment for him, edging its way forward towards the goal he had set for it: eight quarter-miles each in 58 seconds, with a minute's interval between them.

Then, abruptly, the progress stopped; the times refused to go down any further.

Jock saw his panic and said with a grin: "Dinna worry, laddie. You're bored, that's all. Take a while off. Go down to the seaside, run on the dunes a wee, or up mountains if there's any handy. Dinna tie yoursel' tae a schedule. Then we'll see."

XXXIII

Foley and he rented a caravan at Newcastle, the spick-and-span seaside town Beth and he had driven thorough on their very first day. The site was on a flat field a mile north of the town, looking directly across to the mountains where they rose from their shaggy foundations. They were in the corner furthest from the road; between them and the traffic was an assortment of shacks and trailers, permanently temporary. You felt they would stand flimsily there till they fell to pieces. Yet they were well cared for, being the cherished summer lungs of city families.

The field was noisy in the morning as men and women sang while they washed or collected their clinking milk-bottles, delivered to their caravan doorsteps as though it was the most natural thing in the world. Or listening on their transistors to brisk morning music that distance and three-inch loudspeakers reduced to an anonymous scratching.

Colin, bourgeois to the collar stud, found all this strange, even daunting, but to Foley it was as natural as breathing: it was the kind of atmosphere he had grown up in.

Not that either saw much of it; they were out running before most of the others on the site had started breakfast. And when they came back in mid-morning they found the place deserted, its inhabitants having moved off to town, to swim on the beach or in the pool, to throw away their small change in the slot machines, to date the girls.

Lunch and dinner were quiet times; most of their neighbours lived off fish and chips and ice cream in town and never came back to cook. By contrast the early night was noisy as the young men came back from their encounters with Guinness or women, expansive and raucous. They would shout good-natured chaff to each other as they marched up to their doors, as late as three in the morning. They kept Colin awake the first night, but after that he heard none of it, being lost in sleep from nine o'clock.

Brendan and he would be on the dunes by eight in the morning, having breakfasted off some unsavoury fry washed down by strong tea and laughter; they had fetched their running kit from where it had been hanging out to dry on a string between the gable of their caravan and their neighbour's, and they were off.

The dunes were a quarter of a mile away, on the other side of the championship golf links with its narrow fairways, bottomless bunkers and impenetrable heathery rough. They ran on the strip of sand-hills between it and the long strand that stretched away towards the lighthouse at St John's Point.

It was pure pleasure to be out on the tangy seaside morning. They were blessed with bright weather; a fresh breeze swept across the piled-up mountains of sand; sunshine glinted on the marram grass, glossy green when it was young and new, dulled with grey mildew when it grew old. There were, too, banks of gorse—called "whins" in Ireland—pin-cushions of dusty green spines, long since robbed of their yellow blossoms, which children use for staining their Easter eggs.

Once across the last fairway they would leap forward with a yell and set about exhausting themselves. It wasn't difficult; the sand, hard and pleasant to run on where it was bound together by the roots of grass and heather, had slopes into which their feet sank as though into powder: they would toil uphill, refusing to slow down, while the sweat spurted from their pores. But they were free of restraint; they could fly downhill like runaway railway engines, they could do hand-springs or knock each other over in rugby tackles. Their activity, which over the last months had been one steady pounding, now swung wildly

174

between near-rest and exhaustion.

Many famous runners had trained this way, and it was easy to see why. They would stay out for hours on end, getting through far more work than on the track, buoyed up by variety of interest: the changing landscape—dunes, grasses, near villas and distant mountains—and the sky with its towering cumulus for ever evolving into something new and pleasing.

They would come home for lunch between eleven and twelve, bathed in sweat, with fine sand piled in uncomfortable humps in their tennis shoes. After eating—some belly-tightening concoction from tins—they would rest. Foley would study his dentistry books and Colin, in glorious indolence, would doze over some paperback novel.

The sea was a constant delight. On windy days the white-caps would come bellowing in and crash heavily on the shore, staining the sand a darker brown where they fell and leaving small deposits of bubbling foam: Colin could easily imagine the monster sent by Poseidon to frighten the team of Hippolytus, that other incorrigible athlete. And all the time there were the changing levels of blues and greens and the cold, invigorating breath: paternal breath, meant for men-children only. Colin loved the sea at the best of times; now, delirious as he was from the expense of energy, its prospect made him drunk.

One morning they took the bus southwards beyond the town to a place called Bloody Bridge—one of those massacres that stud Irish history had taken place there, but now the only red stain there came from banks of fuchsia—and, in heavy studded boots, raced upwards, over rocks and heather and clumps of wiry grass, towards the summit of Slieve Donard, the highest mountain in the Mournes. As they climbed, the sea behind them became frozen into motionless blue-grey wrinkles flecked with white; the air was heady and light, and they rose into a limitless expanse of ether.

The summit was disappointingly sordid. There was a stone hut, meant perhaps as a shelter but now half filled with boulders: a kind of indoor cairn. Indeed all around was a sea of stones, that rolled unpleasantly underfoot and harboured a variegated refuse: rusty tin cans; labels, dried up and caked with dirt; cigarette packets. That contemporary polluter, the tourist, had passed this way. Colin and Brendan were glad to raise their eyes and follow the course of the massive stone wall that linked Donard to the other summits and delimited the property of the Belfast Water Board.

They came down by a different slope and in due course panted into a luxuriant park, full of ancient trees, that ran down to the Shimna River, whose water brawled over a bed of granite particles, speckled like oatmeal.

"Granite water. The purest in the world," said Warnock to Foley proudly, as though he had invented it.

They crossed the stream on a row of loaf-shaped boulders and toiled up to the little road to Bryansford; here again was a spot he had passed with Beth on that first day. But this time he was going in the opposite direction, downhill instead of up, running instead of motoring, sweating in his heavy boots and stout clothing.

Ten days they stayed in Newcastle; on the last afternoon of June they left. As if on cue, the brilliant weather vanished and a damp mist rolled in from the bay, condensing into a fine drizzle over the town. It was inevitable: tomorrow was the first day of the main holiday month.

The bus to Belfast splashed and hissed along the wet roads. It could not go fast enough for them; suddenly they had had enough of the lotus-eating life. It was desperately important to know what times they would do tomorrow.

XXXIV

But it rained steadily for two whole days, frustrating them. They were reduced to weight training and badminton in the gym. Warnock swore he would go out on the roads come rain, hail or shine; but Jock forbade him. "Do you want to slip and maybe pull a muscle? Damn the road you'll go out on. Tomorrow there's the return meting with Collegians—your old school. You'll want to do well against them, especially after last time."

"All right then, but enter me in the mile."

"Not on your Nellie. The half for you, laddie. But if you want some extra exercise you can have a stab at the four-forty as well."

The following day the sky had lifted and the rain held off. The Collegians match was at Cherryvale: a still-drenched Cherryvale where huge drops fell heavily and unexpectedly from the trees. Colin ran with contained power and beat Foley by three yards in the half.

Thirty minutes later, in wretched conditions, Rex and he took their marks for the four-forty. It was impossible not to think of that previous occasion—a mere eight weeks before—when Hunter had taken revenge for his defeat in training; sudden antagonism flickered between them. Their two opponents looked at each other, puzzled, sensing even worse defeat than they had expected.

The pistol drew all of Colin's recently won strength to a point. He ran with arrogance, breaking Rex's resistance in the fourth hundred. When the time was announced he was not surprised, but took the handshakes and congratulations with aplomb; 46.2 seconds, a new Irish record. Jock hardly dared to think what it might have been on a dry day and on cinders.

"Bastard!" mumbled Rex, giving him a push on the shoulder, half in admiration, half in envy.

Monday's training times confirmed the euphoria. Colin did his eight quarter-miles in fifty-eight seconds without visible effort; he repeated the performance on the next day, and on the day after that. His style was highly gratifying to Jock: hands held low now and shoulders relaxed, he took the curves with no let-up in speed, his leg cadence flexible as the gears of a car.

He had never felt stronger in his life; he had forced his body to the limits of endurance until those limits had become the norm. And he had gained knowledge of his own processes: he knew how far he could push himself, and that that would be far enough. He felt hard and confident; surely now he had done the work, had made the sacrifices? —He would run the mile in three fifty-two and bring home an A.A.A. title.

There was dangerous poetry in running just inside one's limits; you were like a man skirting a precipice but never actually falling over. His body had the strength and cunning to do that; he followed its every movement with loving knowledge.

Jock took him aside and said: "Colin laddie, I've done all I can for you now. You're ready. Keep to your schedule for the next couple of days, then start easing off. I want you fresh for the big occasion."

He did precisely that, holding himself in that delicate state of preparation where strength remains constant but the edge of eagerness is not blunted.

The day before they were due to leave for London, Jock spoke to him again. "Aye, Colin, you can do us proud this time. Physically you're at a pitch I've never seen before in any athlete of mine. Nothing can hurt you as long as you're happy in your own mind; nothing can stop you going out and handing those two buckoes a hiding. Remember, neither of them has got within a second of three fifty-two yet. Just be yoursel' and you'll make the headlines. Aye, and I'll make a wheen of money." His eyes twinkled.

"Mercenary Scot," said Colin laughing. But he thought: yes, you'll make it all right. He *would* win; winning had become no more than his due.

XXXV

The following morning the postman brought an envelope addressed in Schuhmacher's Gothic hand, full of jagged angles and long narrow loops.

Out of it fell the traditional slim volume, as perfectly preserved as if it had come off the press the day before. The cover was of a rich blue-green cloth that looked like watered silk, the creamy pages as stiff as tinfoil; the print had an expensive brownish tinge. Perhaps surprisingly, the print was Roman, but a Roman that was unmistakably Teutonic. Clearly a quality production: had Schuhmacher paid for it himself? Possibly; the imprint was of a Leipzig firm Colin had never heard of. That could denote a vanity publisher, but was perhaps a small specialist house that had gone out of existence after delivering itself of *Der Wind Gottes* by Klaus Schuhmacher.

What of the contents? He leafed over the little book impatiently, trying to take in everything at once. Here was a poem addressed to a marionette—yes, Kleist's marionette: an evocation of the tortured poet stopping at a Punch and Judy show; his flash of inspiration as he watched the strangely graceful movements of these creations of wood, steel and string; and of course the moral: learn the lesson of the puppet, leave yourself open to the direct intervention of the divine will. Uncle Klaus at twenty—yes, a look at the date on the fly-leaf confirmed the age—was the same man as Uncle Klaus at sixty.

The title poem began with a description of a storm in the Harz mountains. Schuhmacher called upon the wind to blow through him with its primitive vigour—but not as Shelley had: the language was dark and portentous, full of abstract nouns. There was little of the direct observation of nature that even a rhapsodist like Shelley was capable of.

Colin, with his budding academic training, looked for influences and found them: Rilke of course, that was unavoidable from a young man writing circa 1930. The priestly Stefan George: Uncle Klaus was clearly flattered by the idea that the poet was a man apart. Not a trace of twentieth century colloquialism, not a trace of withering into truth.

The subjects were typical of a civilisation which has come to prefer the artist's personality to his art: a dramatic monologue *Rimbaud at Harar*, in which the French poet's life was seen as a tormented and cynical flight from his vocation; *Demetrius*, the vision of a play that had killed two great dramatists, Schiller and Hebbel.

There were a couple of perfunctory love poems (more compliments than poems) and a sequence of mild epigrams in elegiac couplets castigating contemporary writers for their small-souled attitude to life.

Judge the poems he must, though they had hardly been sent him with that in mind. He awarded them a Beta Plus. They were skilled but derivative, a respectable first appearance in print but no more. This was no work of genius, not even one of genuine if small talent. Wincing, Colin thought: Klaus was not the man to be satisfied with so little. Hence his suppression of the book all those years.

He turned the volume over in his hands; it was sad and a little ridiculous. He was reminded of Glendower in *Henry IV*:

I can call spirits from the vasty deep.
—But do they come when you do call to them?

Klaus had invoked the wind of heaven, but the wind refused to blow; the genie wouldn't come out of the bottle. Result: the classic discomfiture of the overreacher, the man who disregards the lessons of practical morality: the golden mean, a bird in the hand, don't set your sights too high.

Flaunt that and you're laughed at, inevitably, as Klaus was. As he, Colin, might be too.

Because was he not also flaunting practical morality every time he stepped on to a track? Was he not also claiming the status of an exceptional being? And what happened if his performance made a mockery of that claim?

Practical wisdom lubricated the wheels of the world; but some people were driven to defy it. Schuhmacher was one, he was another. Schuhmacher had made his challenge and lost, and for forty years the world's ghastly laughter had been ringing in his ears. If he, Warnock, failed to justify himself as a runner would that not be his fate too? If on the other hand he succeeded, would that success not bring Klaus an oblique sense of ease? Surely it was that hope which had prompted him to send Colin the poems in the first place? Very well, then; he would run for Klaus as well as for himself.

He was fully defined now: one of the great clan which defies practicality, dedicating itself to the imaginary and the useless. What he did ploughed no field, raised no city; but without the impulse he represented there would be no fields and no cities. His reward: a feeling inside. His punishment for failure: laughter. Both were air, no more.

He thought with grim humour: I'll know which of the two it's to be by twenty past three on Saturday afternoon.

XXXVI

What struck him most about the White City was its size. When Jock and he went round the side to find the competitors' entrance it seemed the grimy wall would never end. They had stood for a moment at the front gate, he digesting his lunch of boiled haddock and watching the anonymous crowd channelling itself through the turnstiles; Jock, beside him, had given a startled look at a newsboy's poster and bought himself an early edition of the *Standard*.

"Holy mackerel!" he exclaimed, "Galliver's not running!"

The sports page proclaimed it: the great Galliver, European champion over fifteen hundred metres, had bruised his toe in training and would not be defending his A.A.A. title. It was not a serious injury, the paper confided, but it would keep him from running for a week or two. The race could now be considered a certainty for the great Russell. There were those who thought the young Irish athlete Warnock might spring a surprise, but that was not this scribe's opinion; the said Warnock had in his view not fulfilled his early promise . . .

"For Christ's sake dinna greet about it," said Jock sharply. "It's only a bleddy journalist. —Anyhow you're better off wi'out that March hare. He's always shooting off unnerving everybody. Russell's easier to handle—just a big strong laddie who'll try to run you into the ground."

But Galliver's defection angered Colin; he had banked on running against this man and now it wouldn't happen.

They shuffled through the entrance and in a moment were in the changing rooms. Dark, dank and smelly, as always; the nose detected man-smell, dust and urine from the toilets, plus Sloan's Liniment and Elliman's Rub. The place was strangely silent too; you could hear absolutely nothing from outside.

Where had the crowd vanished to?

Most of the competitors were there already. As he arrived three of them clumped off down a corridor labelled ARENA. He glanced round; why, he didn't know a single person here! Wait though; there was a great sprinter he'd seen on television. He looked oddly puny here, in need of a square meal. Beside him, a pair of Russians were talking in low voices; further on there was a group of American blacks and then a Sikh who had his hair tied up in a top-knot. He'd never exchanged a word with any of them and was suddenly homesick for the family atmosphere of Ireland.

"Right, laddie," said Jock in an unusually kindly voice, "I'm away to the stand. You're on your own now. —Look, there's Russell coming in now."

A large man, burly for a miler, came in. He had a subdued, gentlemanly hello for half the room. "Good luck mind," added Jock, making for the door. Colin realised he was sweating in his sports jacket and took it off; London, he was discovering, is ten degrees warmer than Belfast. Besides, it was a hot day outside, with a hint of thunder.

A sudden loud crack made him jump: a hulking athlete had been lying on a bench being pummelled by his masseur, a rooster-like man with the unmistakable air of an army P.T. sergeant; this man had caught his charge with a resounding flat-handed smack on the chest to announce that he had finished, and grinned a wolfish grin.

The momentary surprise subsided; they all had their own preoccupations. Low, almost menacing level of voices again, in the margin of silence, until the squeak of a chair leg on the cement floor made them look perfunctorily up again.

Colin was in the act of pulling up his running shorts when a jolly voice came out of a cobwebbed loudspeaker on the wall: "Welcome to the White City, this great national stadium of ours, where you're going to see the cream of British athletes and many others from overseas doing battle for the honour of an A.A.A. title . . ." It was the stadium commentary; the organisers had hired a well-known radio personality to do the job.

So they were starting. That meant the mile would be in forty-five minutes. Jock would be well ensconced now, poring over his programme. He looked at his own; yes, there it was: One Mile, 3:15 p.m. The list of competitors, in alphabetical order, put himself last, with Russell directly above him. Who *were* all these people? G. Hough (Bacup Harriers), R. Higgs (Bolton), B. Longbottom (Bradford)—he'd never heard of one of them; what could they possibly look like?

Then he thought: they're wondering the same about me. We're all provincial athletes, we know what's going on in London but haven't the faintest idea about developments in any peripheral city except our own. The potted biographies at the back revealed that both Hough and Longbottom had bettered four minutes; he felt a new respect for them.

Beside him somebody belched and said: "This bloody diet fills you with wind and piss."

He was engulfed by the hollow weariness that comes before a race. The insistent loudspeaker voice, with its facts and figures and its jolly jokes, flowed over and under and round him, mingling in his head with disjointed phrases from Schuhmacher's poems; the memory of Beth's head turning, bringing its curtain of hair with it; am I to be saddled with a good-for-nothing?

Unsettled, he decided it was time to go out on to the track, to limber up and get used to the crowd. The first trickle of hot and tired competitors started arriving back, to be congratulated or commiserated with. He stood up in track suit and tennis shoes, took his spikes in his hand and made his way towards the door. Somebody, unconcerned, was reading a newspaper: the perfect temperament.

The sign ARENA led into a tunnel, cold, reverberating, sweating drops of moisture even in this weather. His tennis shoes went *squitch!* on the concrete floor. Where was this damned thing leading? It was more like a tunnel in the Underground than the entrance to a sporting arena. When do I come up for air?

He soon found out. Sudden sunlight punished his eyes; he was climbing steps into the centre of a vast square that bewildered him with its size. To the left, the shadow of the stand, a dark gash; to the right, piercing brightness, with summer crowds hanging over the railing, eating their sandwiches. He stood there, blinking.

A white-uniformed steward with gold braid epaulets shouted: "Move along, you there. Shot-putt in five minutes."

He called a second time before Colin realised he meant him. An athlete coming up from the tunnel at that moment grinned and said: "They walk greyhounds when they're finished with us." Colin recognised a famous ten-thousand metres man, an Olympic silver medalist.

A dull pop from a starting pistol: half a dozen young women went dolphining over high hurdles down one side of the track; a blonde won. Colin walked over to the opposite side to look at the running surface; he had heard bad reports of it.

The cinders lay in a broad band outside a built-up kerb; an imaginary line twelve inches outside this measured exactly four hundred and forty yards. It was physically impossible to run less; you would have tripped on the kerb and fallen over. He would have to run further to find the best footing or to draw out and pass a competitor. Five and three quarter inches out, you had to run an extra yard; that meant four yards in the mile. And four yards were four-tenths of a second on your time . . .

This was damned silly; others had exactly the same problem as he had. But his thoughts *would* keep coming back to the time he would lose if he had to go round the bunch instead of sticking to the pole: the difference between a record and just another good time.

It was true; the track wasn't at its best. When he tried it with his spikes he found it looser than it should have been; there wasn't enough clay to bind it. And the inside lane was beginning to break up. He looked involuntarily towards the stand, seeking out Jock. You see, he was saying, this is something I can't do anything about. Ashamed of his own weakness, he found the answer himself: What are you grumbling about? You've been training on grass, haven't you? This surface will be a holiday for you.

He had come out too early, he realised; it was much too soon to doff his track suit and start warming up. He would have to wander round for another fifteen minutes. He felt a sudden slight weakness at the back of his knees.

The crowd gave off a hum like a generator, punctuated from time to time by the machine-gun fire of applause or swelling to a steady ululation at the finish of an event. The commentator's voice was everywhere, relayed with a small time delay from the most distant speakers so that you had the impression of a huge echo. Glib bastard! Colin hated his metropolitan voice, longed for something more innocent and friendly, an Irish voice in short.

He watched the high jump for a while. They had got up to six foot ten and the British jumpers were feeling the strain. An Italian he had seen in the changing room sprang elegantly over the bar, picked himself up out of the pit and smoothed his hair. The photographers ignored him; they were waiting for the Russian record holder, who entered the competition at seven feet. He jumped, the bulbs flashed, they packed up their equipment and pushed past him; as far as they were concerned the event was over.

As they jostled him a troublesome idea was born in his

mind; he wasn't going to do himself justice this afternoon. He pushed it resolutely aside: you always felt like that before a race. But it persisted. He was all alone in this enormous place, weighed down with a heavy burden of responsibility. Self-created responsibility of course, but that did not make it any lighter.

Come, be sensible. He took mental stock of himself: from head to foot, in perfect physical condition. True enough, but the *psychological* condition? He gave himself a shake; this was preposterous. He went over to the unoccupied side of the track again and did a few exercises. Then, with the blood circulating freely, he took off his track suit, made sure his number was firmly attached to his vest and started trotting up and down. The jogging action helped him, made him feel more comfortable. The starter called the competitors for the mile.

He had the outside lane; the people hanging over the rail could almost touch him. He noticed a man eating an apple, a bored-looking girl sitting beside a youth in cavalry twill trousers who was shading his eyes from the glare with his programme. Their nearness was disconcerting; he felt like a condemned man laying his head on the block only to be favoured with an excellent view of the executioner's boots.

He hauled his thoughts by main force back to his own bodily world: the crew of bones, muscles and organs of which his brain was captain. He set his jaw, daring them to let him down.

The starter called their names, his own last. He said "Present!", then narrowed his perception to the square metre of track on which he stood. His memory he concentrated on the hours of training he had done; would they not stand him in good stead now? He had paid the price conscientiously; now was the time to take delivery of the goods ordered: an A.A.A. title and a time of three fifty-two.

From the corner of his eye he looked across to the other runners. They were introverts like himself, their eyes staring blindly at nothing. But were they contemplating an inner relaxation, as Russell seemed to be doing, or a hypertense, convulsive determination like his own? The tiny fragment of his mind that still noticed things had taken in their identities. Higgs was the balding man, Longbottom—astonishingly—that aristocrat in the purple vest . . .

"On your marks." Bodies, wills, reached forward in the familiar way.

"Set." An agonised second, and the pistol fired them into history.

Chapter 4

I

"Let's get things into perspective," said Jock. "It was the fastest mile ever done by an Irishman."

"I lost."

"Dinna cry your eyes out; it won't be the last time."

Warnock gave him an angry look, blowing the air from his nostrils in a voiceless snort.

"Listen, son. You made a deal with me and you're sticking to it. You'll be back at the White City for the August Bank Holiday meeting. It's the Great Britain-France match, with a few extras thrown in. One's an invitation mile; I've an invitation for you in my pocket."

"That should have come to me!" Anger jerked Warnock out of his sulkiness. "What are you doing with a letter of mine?"

"It came to me in the first place. I ran into the Secretary in the stand just after you finished second to Russell and he said he'd like to see you run again. I said he could have you for the Bank Holiday."

"Damned generous of you. What if I decide to run in a local meeting instead?"

"You won't, laddie. And for why? Because you'll be feeling too sore to face people. You'll be damned glad to go to London and get a second chance. —Now enough of this prattle. Brendan and Rex are waiting for us."

Colin was nervous about facing them. About Brendan he

need not have worried; he made no mention of the race, whether from discretion or timidity Warnock didn't know. Perhaps it was even because of his exalted view of athletics: he was unwilling to hurt a man in his faith.

Hunter had no such scruples. He was frankly curious as to Warnock's reaction to the 3:56 mile and a ten-yard beating from the Australian. His gambit was a neat piece of non-commitment. "You did rightly," he said.

Colin gave him a barbed look, ready to take offence if that was possible. But who could take offence at a good-natured idiot like Hunter? He merely said: "Do you think so?"

"It's better than Delany ever did."

"And four seconds slower than I trained for. Damn it all, Rex, you know as well as I do that it was useless."

Hunter shrugged his shoulders. "Ach, there's always another day," he said.

"How very original."

Rex ignored the sarcasm. "What happened anyway? You were fit."

"I didn't run fast enough, that's what happened."

They trained under a warm July sun; rooks cawed in the tree-tops. To Colin's astonishment, he discovered that he was doing first-class times, better than ever before. His body was springing back to competence after punishment as easily as catapult elastic. He was in peak condition; there was no doubt about that. The thought made him absolutely furious.

As he drove away from Cherryvale his mind returned to the White City. The memory of that race had been burned into it like the recollection of some childhood ignominy, one of those moments of cowardice or dishonesty we remember intermittently through life. He dreamt up a hundred excuses, imagined a hundred different endings to the story, but kept crawling back like a beaten dog to the indisputable fact that was his master: when the decisive moment came he had nothing to give. It was a repeat of that other mournful landmark in his life, the Santry race last autumn.

He hadn't the ghost of an excuse. He had given everything in his preparation, had paid and paid into the physical account. But when the moment of withdrawal came the account was empty. He had been cheated, by some flaw in his character perhaps.

Russell wasn't a subtle runner. His sole tactic was to take the lead at the bell and run the last lap flat out, killing the opposition before the finishing straight. Warnock had followed him round like a shadow, so close that his shins were spattered with dirt and cinders kicked up by his spikes, waiting for the inevitable let-up fifty yards from the tape.

The moment came; he recognised it quite clearly. And prepared to draw out and pass an imperceptibly slowing opponent. But couldn't do it. He was completely drained. All he could do was follow his man home, losing ground with every stride.

The London papers commented with surprise on this performance by a little-known Irish athlete. Some predicted a brilliant future for him. This filled him with an agony of shame.

II

But his main emotion was resentment.

He was not the rebellious type; there was never enough energy left over from his personal problems to direct outwards. But revolt was in him now: not the petulance that had made him give up running last autumn, but something more positive and malicious; he was a year older now, at a time when a year counts. But the drudgery of training blunted his temper; when a man has punished his body for four hours in a day provocations don't mean a lot.

Then he came upon Schuhmacher. It was in the Botanic Gardens, in the selfsame place where he had met him months before; but now it was summer. The professor was standing under the tall trees at the College Green entrance, taking the air but avoiding the sun at the same time. Colin came walking past the domed hothouse, newly painted a blinding white and radiating brightness from its panes. It was odd to think of the languorous, oddly vicious plants inside uncoiling themselves in the tropical heat, dripping with humidity, while outside it was a diamond-clear Irish day, neither warm nor cool, with a small wind breathing among the flower beds.

For these nondescript death-barrows of winter were transformed now into pieces of ornamental stucco-work planted with flowers, known and unknown, in baroque patterns. Inside limiting lines of blue lobelia and hoary alyssum with its white pin-point blooms stood the taller massifs: asters like dyed ostrich-plumes, gladioli stiff as wax, in unmixed colours straight from the tube. The whole hummed with insects.

On the lawn to his right, in perambulators and dainty push cars, the babies of the district competed in the daily *concours d'élégance*. Only Schuhmacher, standing in the shade like some myopic bird, reproached the season.

"Good afternoon, Colin. Do you not usually train at this time?"

Warnock suppressed a movement of annoyance. "I was out this morning."

"You haven't come to see me since that London race."

"No."

"It was a setback for you, of course. But not final. Nothing is ever final."

Colin looked him in the eye. "You don't really believe that. At sixty a lot of things are." He kicked a pebble, making it scutter along the macadam and jump neatly into the trailing skirts of a privet bush.

"Are you running again this summer?" The voice was almost pleading. "You tell me nothing."

"I'm going to the White City on Monday week. It's Jock's idea, sending me off to get beaten again."

"Don't be bitter. Not at your age. Give life a chance to work things out. It will, in its own time."

"Wonderful advice from you, I must say."

"I'm only telling you to be patient."

Warnock burst out: "I wish to God you'd stop telling me anything at all! What right have you to live my life for me? You're perpetually on my back, like the old man of the sea. I won't have it! When are you going to realise that we can be friends only if we're equals?"

He turned away, not waiting for an answer. Schuhmacher stood very still, his dark eyes fixed on a tattered notice board bearing the by-laws of the Belfast corporation. He did not feel the cruelty of Colin's reproaches; only their justice.

III

On the Saturday afternoon before Bank Holiday Warnock was walking down University Road. He was on light training now, tapering off before the race. Not that the race preoccupied him much; it was one of those irksome things one can't avoid, like a class test.

It was a dull day. The city had lost the working purpose that gave it its identity; apart from an occasional lost soul pushing a pram there seemed to be nobody about. The red buses ploughed emptily on their errands, their conductors hanging on to the handrail and yawning.

A tall, intent figure emerged from Sandy Row with a newspaper, folded into eight and smudged grey from handling, stuffed into his jacket pocket. It was Sam Harbinson.

"Hullo. Where have you been?"

Harbinson patted the newspaper and jerked his eyebrows in the direction from which he had come. "Bookie's. Felt like a gargle before investing in the four-thirty. —I'd stand you one only you're in training." His sallow cheeks cracked in a sardonic smile.

All Warnock's frustrations and resentment focussed on the fact that he couldn't have a drink when he wanted one. "To hell with training," he said. "I'm with you."

They walked back up the road to Mick's and perched on a pair of high stools at the bar. A perfectly round man of about fifty with a moon-shaped, intelligent face said: "Gentlemen?" The accent was vaguely southern; he wore a black overall with the sleeves rolled up to the elbows.

"Pint of draught Guinness. —What about you, Warnock?"

"Half of lager." Revolt was still a new-born babe; and anyway he didn't like stout.

Harbinson put the black column of porter, crowned with its yellow disc of froth, to his head and poured half of it down his throat at a gulp. Then he wiped his upper lip, sucked his teeth and said: "That hits the spot."

Not to be outdone, Colin took a long pull at his lager. It was fizzier than the draught; he could only get a third of it down. He belched discreetly into his hand.

The preliminaries over, Harbinson said curtly; "When's your next race?"

"Day after tomorrow."

"Hm. Against who?"

"Galliver—you know, the European champion. Horvath of Hungary. An American called Lenehan. And a few others."

"They're slave-driving you. You were out a week or two ago. Some Aussie beat you."

"Yes."

They finished their drinks; the beer was cold on the stomach but Colin found it starting to relax him. Harbinson stared into his glass, ringed with muddy froth, and placed it on the counter.

"Same again, gents?"

"Why not?" said Colin.

Harbinson held up his hand. "Time enough. First: the bookie's."

They walked back down the road and turned left into Sandy Row, a twin line of red houses that undulated like a sine-curve traced in brick. A short way down it, on the right, Harbinson led the way through an anonymous door into a concrete-floored room with a wooden partition down one side; this was pierced by three small windows with apron counters along which a couple of shuffling men were at that moment sliding little piles of silver and coppers. Half-concealed clerks gave them betting slips in exchange.

The other walls were covered with pinned-up pages from racing papers. Weird headlines screamed at them: "THE SCOUT SAYS PILLOW TALK." "TWINKLE TOES FOR KEMPTON." "THERSITES ON THE NOSE." Colin thought; the astonishing names men give to horses.

Most of the papers gave, in tabular form, the selections of all the tipsters. In some races there was broad agreement between them, in others the wildest variations. It was clear why the bookmaker, not the punter, was in business.

"I didn't even know this place existed," said Warnock.

"That's the beauty of this city. You can get anything you want if you're in the know."

"What horse are you on?"

Harbinson waved a disdainful hand at the papers on the wall. "Nothing these guys have tipped. A nag called April Shower. I know a man who's married to the jockey's sister. It'd better come up; I'm a quid down today already."

Colin examined his watch: four twenty-seven. The beer sang gently inside him. "When will you know?"

"Straight away; they have a line to the course. But this one is televised as well, and there's a set in the pub next door. We can go there if you like. No? —You're right. Why bother? Let the mountain come to Mohammed."

Colin let this oracular statement pass and examined the other people in the betting shop. There were ten or twelve of them, all men. Pasty-faced youths with pimply chins and slicked-down hair: depressed clerks or counter-hoppers. Big florid-faced men with an air of black dustiness: coal-heavers perhaps. And broken-down ancients in clothes green with age and dirt, their whole persons radiating senility and grime; they had battered hats and bleary eyes, their hands trembled as they turned the pages of the racing papers, and they clearly had no money to bet with. They came here because they had nowhere else to go, not even the public park; God alone knew how they ate or where they found a bed. Their best hope was that some euphoric winner would toss them a sixpence.

"Here they come," said Harbinson. With that a wave of cloth-capped men burst through the door brandishing dockets and laughing with pleasure. "They've been next door looking at the box. —What won, mate?"

"April Shower."

"What price?"

"A hundred to six."

Harbinson took his triumph coolly. "In this game you have to have connections," he said. "I had five bob on that pony, at just over fourteen to one. That makes three pound ten in winnings: a good day."

"And I owe you a drink."

"You do at that."

Unusually for him, Colin was finding life richly funny; back in the pub every remark of Sam's, however trite, had him on the verge of laughter. After the first beer it became the most natural thing in the world to accept a second. He soon had to go to the lavatory and was surprised to find himself walking with a slight lunging movement. This too amused him; he gave an audible titter.

He returned to the acrid taste of hops on the palate, drinking with mingled disgust and pleasure, a disgust that was in itself pleasure; was this the drunkard's secret? His belly was a half-filled water bottle slapping around inside him.

The porter made no impression on Sam's severity. He explained with total seriousness: ". . . that made ten bob down. But I had the first leg of a double up, and if Thersites had won the three-thirty I'd have been three-ten to the good. I should have known better; Lamming was up. That crook wouldn't ride a straight race on a donkey on the sands. Photo finish naturally. Catch him making it obvious! So bang went my double. Mind you, I had hedged with an each-way bet on Cream Cracker and that saved me a bit. But I came down like a ton of bricks in the four o'clock . . ."

Colin was no longer listening. The fizz of the beer had deadened his sense of hearing; he floated away on its fumes like a man in a hot bath, nodding his head sagely. He realised with surprise that he would have to go to the lavatory again. Swaying back on his seat he suddenly announced: "I'm hungry. No, I'm not—I'm bloody starving. Let's go somewhere."

"Don't move." Harbinson raised an admonitory hand. "No need to leave the premises."

"Nonsense. All they have is cashew nuts."

"They have a telephone." Stiff as a ramrod, he walked across to the booth. Colin heard him say ". . . Fish and chips for two. . . . I'm in the pub across the street. No it's not a joke . . . Certainly I'll pay. If I don't you can always take them back again . . . In two minutes. Right." He came back, shrugged and said: "There you are."

A thin old man in a check cap and steel-rimmed spectacles had come in and was nodding over his stout, foam from his first draught still quivering on the yellow ends of his moustache. As Warnock and Harbinson raised their glasses he said in a complaining voice: "Youse young ones have it easy. Nothing to do but raise your elbows. When I was your age I had ten cows to milk every evening and then I had to walk home five miles for my supper."

"Hard cheese, granda," said Sam. "And I'm not talking about the cows."

"Many's the day I wrought from six in the morning till eight at night. First the cows. Then the gardens. Then the reaping. And I had to draw fifty buckets of water from the well because we had no pumps in them days . . ."

His monologue petered out for lack of listeners; Harbinson had slopped some of his porter on the counter and was shaping it with his finger into a map of Ireland. Colin watched with inane interest. Only the round-faced barman nodded his sympathy. "I'm a country lad myself," he said. "From down beyond Dundalk."

A dark-haired boy of twelve or thirteen appeared at the door with a brown paper parcel. "Are youse the ones that wanted the fish suppers?"

"We're the ones," said Harbinson, holding out the money. Colin and he fell upon the food. The fat hot slices of potato and greasy batter-crisp fish were a benediction to their taste-buds. They ordered a third helping, again by telephone ("I never move when I'm settled," said Sam) and shared it between them.

Time passed imperceptibly. "Good heavens, it's nearly seven," said Colin, looking at his watch.

"We'll soon be getting the Saturday night crowd in. The sports programmes are over and they'll have had their tea."

"I'm going to have to stop. I can't hold any more."

"Change to shorts. You can't drink that fizzy muck all night. Here, Michael, give the man a Scotch and soda."

People started to drift in, including a small business-like man in black boots and an old serge suit. He talked his way up to the bar. "Grand night, boys. Heh-heh, but it's grand to see the rain houldin' off. Stout, Michael. You know my bad habits, heh-heh. Man but that's a brave night."

The whisky made Colin catch his breath. The malt taste, mingled with that faint nausea all distilled liquours give off, dispelled the cloudy atmosphere of the beer. But it was a tem-porary clarity only; in a moment the porter casks and rows of liqueur bottles behind the bar had started to dance, filling him with a fierce wobbly delight in being himself. He was Colin Warnock, and that was good thing to be. He slapped Sam on the shoulder, amicably patronising. "This is great bloody stuff," he opined.

The bar began to fill. A newsboy irrupted, carrying a bundle of sporting papers under his arm, and made a whirlwind tour, pocketing money and returning the change with bewildering speed. "Second!" he shouted. "Ulster Second, sir?"

Colin bought a copy and looked for the athletics results. Queen's had been engaged earlier that day, but he had been left out of the team because of the London race. Foley and Hunter had won. Of course. But what of the others? Oh, to the devil with the others! This print was too damned small.

He sat on his stool with the paper dangling from his hand. The bar swayed gently around him. He felt that some glorious climax was about to occur and that he would be the star of it. Having no experience of drink, he wondered what it would be. So long as it wasn't sickness! He laughed quietly to himself. Harbinson winked knowingly to the fat barman.

Suddenly the doors were flung open and a troop of young men came in, neatly clad and with their hair slicked back: just out of the shower. They carried long cricket bags. "Come in, Dungannon, I know your knock," one of them observed to Harbinson. They made for the circular snug by the door, which had just been vacated, heaved their bags under the green leather bench and plonked their elbows on the round table with its single steel leg.

"Service!" they cried happily.

Colin, taking another sip at his whisky, felt it burning its way down, like acid. Its fiery exhalation made him stagger, but increased his sense of euphoria.

The cricketers invited Harbinson to join him. He dragged Colin with him into a controlled roar of conversation.

". . . that umpire must be blind. I clicked with my tongue and he gave the batsman out caught . . ."

". . . just my luck. It pitched on a rut and cut in at me. That pitch hasn't seen a roller since Pussy was a cat . . ."

". . . that googly of mine flummoxed him completely. In fact, if he'd been a better batsman he'd have been out. But he never even got a touch. . ."

". . . the main thing is, we won. That gives us an average of 62.5 percent. We'll get promoted if we keep on playing the way we did the day . . ."

The talk flowed over him. He took in phrases here and there, with intense amusement. It wan't the type of joke one needs to share; it was enough just to sit there grinning to himself. Meanwhile the cricketers set about the business of getting drunk. They were going to a hop at nine and had to be reeling by then. Eleven high glasses of porter stood on the table in front of them, gleaming like columns of ebony. Colin decided that they were beautiful in a meaningful way that he had never experienced before. He closed his eyes, bemused by the ineffable.

The cricketers were drinking ever faster. Their voices became more raucous, their movements less predictable. Porter was splashed over the table; one of them put the glass to his head with abandon, and twin squirts of black fluid ran from the corners of his mouth. Colin observed them in owlish silence, taking just enough of the whisky to stay floating on air.

Finally he realised that someone was addressing him. It was the man on the other side of Harbinson; his name, he recollected, was Scab. "Will *you* have one this time?" Scab was saying.

Between them, Harbinson was vociferating at someone on the other side of the snug: "Left half. He played left half."

"Thanks, Scab. I will."

"*Right*-half." The man opposite shook his head violently, as though he'd got a flea inside.

"*McNab*. Bobby McNab."

"*Left*-half," insisted Harbinson. "For Wolverhampton Wanderers."

Colin was nonplussed. "Mac what?"

"*McNab*."

"Who the hell is McNab?" Colin's sudden bellow shocked the others into silence.

"*I* am." It was the man who'd just offered him a drink. "I'm Bobby McNab. What's your name?"

Colin was struck dumb, but Harbinson looked up and said

dismissively: "Oh him? He's Colin Warnock. You know, the great runner." He burst into a rasping laugh.

Embarrassment turned to indignation. "Hold it a minute," he said, "I'm not going to be a great runner for anybody." He looked around him; the cricketers' faces were swelling to enormous size and then deflating.

"You're damned right you're not."

There was another silence.

"Just what do you mean by that?" said Warnock in as icy a voice as he could muster.

Harbinson looked defiantly round the snug and said a little wildly—perhaps even he was getting drunk: "The great bloody runner. What are you doing here then? Get out and bloody well run."

Colin's months of frustration rose intoxicatingly in him. He punched Harbinson deliciously on the jaw, and laughed to see him sprawl across his neighbours.

His head cleared. He was filled with exultation, as though he had smashed through some imprisoning wall and pitched forward into fresh air and freedom. A spring of aggression was released in him, a pure battle-joy. The sensation was so exquisite that he turned to the cricketer on his left and punched him too. Morally indefensible, of course, but he'd think about that later. For the moment moral considerations were out. Life had become laughter.

In a moment the snug had grown writhing arms and legs. The black porter columns shattered on the floor in a welter of glass daggers; the frothy liquid played around the milling feet. The cricketers were all trying to lay drunken hands on Colin but kept getting in each other's way. They started fighting amongst themselves.

In the bar the other drinkers got to their feet, drawing the skirts of invisible overcoats clear of the fray. The small round barman dived under the hinged leaf of the counter and made for the snug. In a moment he had started flinging bodies out of it, by the scruff of the neck; he was as strong as a small bull. "Do you want to have the police in on me, you young rapscallions?" he cried as each offending cricketer emerged.

Colin, who had worked his way into the corner, was last. "You innocent looking ones," said Mick grimly. "You're always the worst." The pudgy fist with iron sinews fastened on Colin's coat collar.

"Wait a minute," he gasped. "It's my fault, I'll pay for the damage. Just let me write down my name and address."

The fist remained in place but granted him access to pencil and paper.

When he had finished writing the barman looked at it round-eyed. "Glory be to God! Brawling in a public house, and you bearing a name like that."

This aspect of the case had not struck Colin. He thought for a moment and said: "The old bugger would have been delighted."

"Away out of this and behave yourself," retorted Mick, scandalised, and put the piece of paper in his pocket.

As Colin emerged into the twilight he found the cricketers standing on the pavement in a loose group; they were clearly in two minds whether to continue the argument. Fortunately a pair of stubby arms gave the fuddled Harbinson the bum's rush and followed that up by flinging their sopping cricket bags on the pavement with a crash. They laughed.

"Come on, lads," said Colin. "How about another up the road? It's on me."

Even Harbinson said yes.

Some time after midnight Warnock clumped into his house. He was as tired as a dray horse that has pulled a cart over cobbles all day, but had strength enough for one symbolic action.

He took the schedule that Jock had given him five months before, tore it in pieces and flushed it down the lavatory. The sight of it being swept away in the cascading water caused him such satisfaction that he hummed the Grand March from *Aida* before falling into bed. Mrs McArdle, who had been wakened by the noise, pulled the bedclothes round herself in alarm.

He woke next morning with an aching head and badly bruised knuckles; they went to London with him as part of his baggage. They were spiritual baggage too: the visible signs of the great peace that had entered his soul. He didn't care a damn about anyone or anything. Jock was puzzled and rather elated by his behaviour.

IV

Six of them lined up for the start of the mile. It was a completely neutral day, neither cool nor warm, neither wet nor dry; shorthand for weather. The crowd made its steady subdued roar like a distant waterfall.

Two of the six were runners Warnock had beaten three weeks before: Higgs and Longbottom. He spoke to them in the changing room like old friends. They knew they had no chance of winning: "We've come for the trip," they said. But he wondered idly whether one or both hadn't an arrangement to fix the pace for Galliver.

Not that it mattered; it wasn't the sort of thing to worry him now. A subtle change had taken place in his character, like a land subsidence which alters old landmarks and creates new ones. The new feature was enjoyment; he had realised the surprising truth that he was a creature well fitted to enjoy. Astonishing but true; in all his years of running he had never positively enjoyed a race. How he had envied the sprinters, the jumpers, the shot-putters, whose events demanded less ascetic discipline than his own! He had seen putters reading the paper or chatting to opponents between throws. And felt excluded. It occurred to him now that he had been excluding himself.

Well, he wasn't excluding himself any more. In a flash of intuition he realised why: he had abjured ambition, the tyranny of schedule and stop-watch, the profit and loss accounting of his training to date. He swore an inward oath: I hereby renounce all side-considerations, all hope of gain or celebrity, retaining one thing only, the satisfaction of doing the thing for its own sake. Foley was said to offer up his running to his favourite saint. Well, he would offer up his to an unspecified divinity: the spirit of running perhaps.

Horvath was in the lane beside him—another old friend, smiling at him, running his hands up and down his bow legs, black with hair.

There were two newcomers. First Lenehan, a stringy young American of his own age, with soft blond hair cut short and sticking out all over in a pad of floppy bristles. He had the engaging American monkey face, the face one sees in films about teenagers. "I'm Irish too," he said. "Second generation American. My old man still marches in the Saint Patrick's Day parade. I'm going to take a look at the old country this trip."

Then, most importantly, the European champion Galliver. Colin looked at him with interest. He was a man of twenty-six, which was getting on for a miler these days, with a body like whipcord. Enormously talented, he had one important failing: his reflexes ran away with him. He had spoiled race after race through impatience.

Colin had seen the film of the last Olympics when Galliver was twenty-two and at the height of his powers. You could positively see the man getting edgy as the runners took the bell and swung into the long semi-circle leading to the back straight. Four hundred yards from home he could stand the strain no longer and made his break, tearing into the lead and electrifying the crowd. He burned himself out before the finish and stumbled across the line in fourth position.

But in the European championships two summers ago the miracle had occurred; he contained himself until fifty yards out, then produced an explosive burst and won. The reason, as the film demonstrated, was that he had been boxed in. He was an anarchic influence; other runners hated having him with them in a race. He made them as jumpy as himself. They tended to lose their sense of pace through worrying about what he was going to do.

Waiting now for the race to start, Galliver rolled his shoulder blades in a circular movement and wrung his hands. The skin of his square face seemed to be pulled too tight over his cheek-bones, fixing his lips in a convulsive smile. He had curly brown hair and was popular off the track.

The starter, having checked their identities, was calling them to their positions. From the inside it was Horvath—Lenehan—Longbottom—Warnock—Higgs—Galliver. Colin felt his chest constrict and his mouth go dry; he was keyed up. But not unpleasantly; he felt like a war-horse when it hears the bugle. There was going to be a fight and he was going to enjoy it. His skin began to prickle.

"Take your marks!"
"Set!"
The pistol.

As he swept forward in line with the others a controlled jubilation came over him. Christ, I'm full of running, I'm absolutely full of it! The richness of his possessions embarrassed him; he hardly knew how to dispose of them all. He would have to spread them out over the full four laps.

Higgs had gone straight into the lead and was spanking along at a good pace. Colin reined himself in easily and floated round in last position, without any sense of effort. In the narrow grey world he was now inhabiting he felt: I am working up to an important conclusion, a moment that must on no account be spoiled. Technique was the important thing; the manner of doing, the professionalism of it. There were no other considerations, whether economic, moral or aesthetic.

They completed the first hieratic circle. Higgs still led, with Horvath trundling bandy-legged behind him; then Lenehan, wiry and elastic; then the withdrawn Longbottom striding along in a solipsistic world—Colin saw that he was no racer but purely a runner, and a Narcissus among runners at that; he ran for the pleasure of watching himself move.

Directly in front of Colin was Galliver; he was able to watch him most clearly of all. The man ran with crude, ill-directed energy, radiating nervous tension. Colin thought: a week ago I would have been affected by this.

As they passed the finishing line for the first time he said to himself: about fifty-eight seconds. Perfect pace. The big dial with its sweeping hand confirmed his estimate. His edge of pleasure grew keener.

There was something mesmeric about their movement. The others, too, had realised that the pace was right; there was no need to disturb the man who was doing the hard work. So they let Higgs pull them round again. With each yard covered the inevitability of running in this particular race strengthened; they grew into it, felt at home together. Every inch of distance was a small bronze weight added to the force that pushed them forwards; momentum increased with the distance covered. This was one of the joys of doing something supremely difficult; each step taken over the elected terrain made the next one easier and more natural.

At the end of the second lap they sensed that they had passed the summit. From now on they were on the downward slope. Colin guessed the time right again: another fifty-eight. This was almost dangerously close to his own wishes. A tiny doubt germed in his mind; was it too good to be true? He brushed it aside as inessential. The only essential thing was this living organism striding round a track and this poised personality, shorn of attributes, ready for its convulsion.

Higgs was beginning to falter; the other athletes smelt it in the air. His manner of running, the very set of him, betrayed uncertainty. Colin's suspicion was correct; he had gone out knowing he had one thing to do, to run a fast first half. Having done that he was free, without a shell of responsibility to fit himself into, like a hermit crab. He was wavering before their eyes.

The pace slackened. The hypnotic effect slowed too, deprived of its rhythm. Runners and crowd came visibly out of their trance and looked around for someone who might lead the way back into it. With what consciousness remained uncommitted to the pressure gauges of heart and lungs, the revolution counters of arms and legs, Colin wondered whether he shouldn't take over the lead himself, but desisted. Why be impatient? Impatience was a characteristic of the Warnock of a few days ago, not the new one.

Galliver too won the struggle with himself and made no move. The entered into a period of temporary *status quo*: a caretaker period in which things stayed as they were until the force of circumstance should alter them. At reduced speed they crawled their way round the great quarter-mile ellipse, like ants on some pointless errand.

At last, when the rate of advance seemed unbearably slow, Lenehan skipped round the two men in front of him and set out on his own. He did it reluctantly; you sensed him looking over his shoulder all the time, praying for someone to help him out, so that he wouldn't hold the lead at the critical moment, a furlong from home.

They came stolidly down the straight to the bell, settled into the new scheme of things. The lap had cost them sixty-one seconds; the clock stood at 2:57. Colin thought; there *must* be a break soon, otherwise the time would be a slow one, another 3:56. He didn't want it to be 3:56; he had passed that stage. But he resolutely put such accountancy out of his mind. What did time matter anyway? It was the race that mattered.

The brash clangour of the bell, riding over the slow crescendo of noise from the crowd, made change imperative. The psychology of the race demanded it. Colin saw Horvath move up to Lenehan's elbow, to have the American as a springboard when he needed one. And now Galliver too was making a move. In a couple of nervy strides he passed Higgs and Longbottom and was in third place. So be it, thought Colin with a pang of excitement. Better have those two behind me where they can do no harm. He passed them too and was ran in the very spike marks of Galliver.

They swept round the long swinging bend. It was a delicious, frightening moment. You knew yourself to be on the verge of the last act—comedy or tragedy? Did it matter anyway? Provided the great mechanism was wound up and given its freedom, the result was of little importance. They were in the play-realm now, the realm of experience heightened by its limitations, its selectivity, and the culminating point of that experience was at hand. They were part of a work of art.

Suddenly, without ceremony, the last act began. Galliver bolted round Lenehan and Horvath, a hare making a dash for safety. There were three hundred yards to go.

Colin had no hesitation; he followed him. Horvath and

Lenehan disappeared behind and to his left. His life, he felt, had been tending towards this single moment. In the heat of the moment it was impossible, unnecessary, to disentangle motives, but he knew subconsciously that he was acting in accordance with his own estimate of himself. The risk was huge but he claimed the freedom to take it. He was saying in effect: in this company I am the best man and I challenge you to dispute it.

Galliver ran, Colin behind him. They were moving very fast, almost at capacity, he realised. How close to himself in ability this man Galliver was! They were both on the verge of total commitment, yet the gap between them never altered. They flung themselves into the last bend as though locked together.

The bend seemed endless; eternally they would be swinging round, inches to the left with every stride, running just within exhaustion; nothing would ever change. Colin was oblivious of the others now; by following Galliver he had dismissed them. These two were the only protagonists now.

As they entered the straight they crossed yet another boundary, into pure physicality. Nothing mattered now but to keep going. Emotional, intellectual commitment were as total as the physical; all that remained was to fulfil those commitments to the end.

Galliver was weakening! This *alter ego*, this twin, was giving up the struggle, worn down prematurely by his own psychology. Colin could see him waver as he ran by the kerb-stone. He was finished.

And a second realisation came, at the level of the blood: a kind of creative orgasm. A great release had taken place in him, unbidden. He knew in theory what it must be: the tapping of the final reserve. But the fact obliterated all theory by its intensity.

It was a wave of feral aggression, a lust for power, and at the same time a sacred terror as though he was being pursued by furies. He exulted and shook with terror at the same time.

Life existed now only as far as the finishing tape, seventy yards ahead. Reaching that, he would put himself beyond the clutch of whatever it was pursued him, and take possession of a glittering kingdom. But it must be done immediately, and he must destroy himself in the process. He must be burnt up in a pyre of his own energy. Shortening his stride, he sprinted past Galliver.

Now there were only himself and the line of white. He felt himself going faster and faster with every step, but at the same time he was slowing to motionlessness. He was a runner in a frieze, the lover in Keats's Ode, forever astrain and forever doomed to remain on the same spot. Time expanded and contracted simultaneously. In this heraldic play-world where all was pregnant with momentous seriousness, a seriousness on the threshold of physical agony, where the actions of this one man who was himself were in some way determining the fate of all men, none of the rules of life applied any more. There was no good, no evil, no success, no failure. There was only the man eternally running, eternally motionless.

Yet, somehow, the tape approached. At one moment it was a mile away, at the next it was before him, breaking against him, he was safe and in his kingdom. And his body was burnt away; it fell away from him, consciousness fell away from him in a change that might have been into life or death or both. But he felt with his last remnant of awareness that arms were receiving him.

He came to into a world of human solidarity, where his fellow men were holding him, taking care of him. It was delicious to feel the texture of a track suit against his face, feel a wiry arm holding him under the shoulders, hear with the return of that sense the tired voices of Lenehan, Horvath, Galliver congratulating him. Their faces were drawn and drained, their cheeks congested, their lips coated with white fur; but they were congratulating him. In his heart he said: I did it for you; in reality, only for you.

The loudspeaker voice penetrated to him; "First, Number Five, C. Warnock of Queen's University, Belfast. Time: three minutes fifty-two point six seconds, which subject to ratification is a new United Kingdom National, United Kingdom All-Comers and European record . . ." A roar, obliterating the voice.

". . . Horvath of Hungary. Three minutes fifty-three point nine seconds.

"Third, Number Two, J. Galliver of Birchfield Harriers. Time; three minutes fifty-four point five seconds.

"Fourth, R. Lenehan . . ."

He hardly knew what these strange facts meant.

Epilogue

The day after Colin arrived back from London he received a telegram consisting of a single word: CONGRATULATIONS. There was no signature, otherwise he would have thrown it on the pile with the others. Instead, he studied the jumble of letters and figures that preceded his name and address, and made out the word FIRENZE.

Firenze! That stood for the future. He drove straight into town and booked himself a flight to Milan, with a connecting train to Florence. It being the holiday season he could get nothing earlier than Friday, two days ahead.

Coming out of the travel agent's he met Schuhmacher, on his way to a second-hand book shop in Smithfield; he had been alerted to some newly arrived volumes.

"Why, Colin, my boy," he said, speaking in English instead of the usual German; the fact deprived him of his tutelary aura. "What a pleasure to read about your win."

The word *read* was a reproach. Colin merely said: "I'm glad you were pleased."

Schuhmacher waved a hand towards the travel agent's. "Are you going somewhere?"

"Fiesole. *Pensione dei Fiori*."

"I think I can guess . . . But the running season is not yet over, is it?"

"No. I'm having a short holiday. I don't think even Jock can object to that now."

"You know best. You are master of the situation now, Colin, and I'm glad. —Which way are you going?"

"Home."

"Then I shall leave you. When are you travelling?"

"Friday morning."

"May I see you off?"

"The plane leaves at twenty to nine. Isn't that a bit early?"

"No. I shall be there."

Colin watched him walk away, incongruous in his Harris tweed sportscoat and flannel trousers. Smaller too, somehow; more shrunken. Perhaps that was a result of his own new maturity; for maturity, he realised, was the prize he had been seeking all along. Did maturity shrink even the strongest personalities to one's own size? Was that how you recognised it?

He wondered whether Schuhmacher had ever achieved it. He too had wanted to do what Colin had somehow managed: to wring the last drop of potentiality from himself and offer it up as a gift to his fellow men. But he had not succeeded. Did that mean he was less mature than Warnock himself? Hardly. Surely *his* maturity was living with this ultimate frustration and turning it into a sardonic triumph of his own?

As for himself, he had uncovered the startling fact that he was one of the fortunate ones, those permitted to express themselves in their own chosen way. He had stumbled on that through the accident of a bar-room scuffle (he still hadn't paid the bill). That had been a psychological lever, in its way an act of grace. Ultimately, he thought, you were driven back to religious language. Grace. Yes, he owed his strenuous salvation to an act of grace.

But grace alone couldn't do it. It was merely an instrument for casting out inessentials: ambition, the thought of reward. It enabled you to travel light. Before it in time came dedication, discipline.

In the play-realm, where no taxes are paid and no votes cast, where the principles of accountancy do not apply, there was only one rule: do your work, forget payment and wait.

Wait for the act of grace, which may or may not come. But at least there is the chance.

There was wind and rain on Friday morning. Lough Neagh lay under a piled ceiling of cloud, and a clammy wind from it drove gusts of stinging rain over the runway. Schuhmacher and he had their winter coats on, but they were chilled.

As they waited in the lounge the professor said to him: "Good luck for your trip. It will be a happy one, I know. And you will both come and see me when you get home."

"Thank you very much."

He laid a hand on Warnock's sleeve. "I have a small fear, Colin. You are not thinking of giving up your running, are you?"

"Of course not. The Olympics are in four months. I'll be starting serious work for them when I get back."

"I am glad. I should not like to think of you giving a thing up after a first small triumph."

"I won't be like that." His voice had an edge of hardness to it: no, by heaven, he was the holder of the United Kingdom National, All-Comers' and European records for the mile; he had also been timed over fifteen hundred metres and held some records there too but had forgotten which. He was certainly not giving up now.

Yet how unreal they were, these honours that the profit-and-loss world awarded to the other kingdom, the more important one: out of admiration, concealed jealousy or as a sop to men who had entertained it for a moment? He neither knew nor cared why. The only reality was the race itself. He thought: let me never cling to the empty honour, the parchment with my name inscribed, the Olympic medal.

"I daresay you will be getting married before long." Schuhmacher sighed. "It will be hard to think of you as head of a family. I used to take you on my knee."

"Strange how I used to think you couldn't have both things together."

"Not strange," said Schuhmacher sadly. "I told you that."

Colin looked up. "You did, now I think of it. But I agreed. We were both wrong."

"My days of telling you things are over, it would seem."

There was no possible reply to that. Luckily the flight was called at that moment. Standing at the glass door waiting to leave, he remembered something. "Oh by the way, Klaus. Could you tell Maxwell to put father's life on hold for a bit? I may want to try it myself."

In a moment the little yellow bus, its panes blind from the beating rain, had taken him out to the aircraft. He scurried up the gangway and made his way to his seat. From his porthole he could make out Schuhmacher's figure at the window; then another gust obscured it.

Down here he was still in a world of sombre monochrome, but in a little while the orange-tipped propeller blades would carry him up, through banks of grey and white fluff, into a universe of startling blue and sunshine, of glittering castles of cloud.